JOIN THE FUN
IN CABIN SIX . . .

KATIE   is the perfect team player. She loves competitive games, planned activities, and coming up with her own great ideas.

MEGAN   would rather lose herself in fantasyland than get into organized fun.

SARAH   would be much happier if she could spend her time reading instead of exerting herself.

ERIN   is much more interested in boys, clothes, and makeup than in playing kids' games at camp.

TRINA   hates conflicts. She just wants everyone to be happy . . .

AND THEY ARE! Despite all their differences, the Cabin Six bunch are having the time of their lives at CAMP SUNNYSIDE!

Too Many Counselors

Marilyn Kaye

AN AVON CAMELOT BOOK

CAMP SUNNYSIDE FRIENDS #8: TOO MANY COUNSELORS is an original publication of Avon Books. This work has never before appeared in book form.

AVON BOOKS
A division of
The Hearst Corporation
105 Madison Avenue
New York, New York 10016

Copyright © 1990 by Marilyn Kaye
Published by arrangement with the author
Library of Congress Catalog Card Number: 90-92980
ISBN: 0-380-75913-6
RL: 5.0

First Avon Camelot Printing: July 1990

For Susan and Simon Golec

Too Many Counselors

Chapter 1

On a bright Monday morning, the cabin six girls were heading back to their cabin after breakfast. The blazing sun beat down on them, and they moved slowly.

Their counselor, Carolyn, was several paces ahead of them. She turned her head and called, "C'mon girls, you're lagging. Hurry up."

"It's too hot to walk fast," Katie said.

"You seemed to have plenty of energy back in the dining hall," Carolyn replied in a sharp voice. "Really, Katie, aren't you a little old to be having food fights?"

"We always have a couple of good food fights every summer," Katie pointed out.

"There was nothing good about it," Carolyn retorted. "And you certainly didn't have to start it."

"Katie always starts food fights," Megan said, giggling. "She's got a reputation to uphold."

1

Carolyn didn't laugh. "Well, I don't see why a person should be proud of a reputation like that."

"What a grouch," Katie muttered to Trina.

Trina could almost agree. Carolyn hadn't been in the best of moods lately. "Maybe it's the heat." She could feel the beads of perspiration on her forehead. "I can't wait to get into the pool today. That water is going to feel good."

"What are we doing in swimming today?" Megan asked, pushing her frizzy red curls away from her face.

"Backstroke," Katie told her.

"Oh, yuck," Sarah moaned. "That's the hardest one for me. I can't get the rhythm right."

"I'll help you," Trina offered, and Sarah shot her a grateful look.

Erin didn't look pleased with the prospect of a backstroke lesson. "I wish it was a free swim day so I wouldn't have to go in the water."

"But it's so hot," Trina said. "Don't you want to cool off?"

"I'd rather lie on the side of the pool and work on my tan," Erin replied. She looked down worriedly at her bare legs. "Do you think it's fading?"

No one bothered to answer that. Katie turned to Trina and rolled her eyes. Trina grinned and nodded. Everyone knew that Erin was totally preoccupied with her looks.

2

"Are you going to wear that bikini you bought yesterday in Pine Ridge?" Sarah asked Erin.

"Why should I?" Erin asked, sighing. "There's no one here to look at me. Except Darrell."

At the sound of their handsome swimming coach's name, the other girls each automatically placed a hand over her heart and pretended to swoon.

"But maybe I'll wear it anyway," Erin said with a teasing grin. "Just to make you guys jealous."

Trina laughed. They all accepted the fact that Erin had the best figure in the group. "I'm sure we'd all be green with envy. It's too bad you can't wear it. You know we all have to wear our tank suits."

Erin made a face. "I hate those awful things. Carolyn?"

Their counselor turned to her. "What?"

"Can I wear my new bikini today?"

Carolyn shook her head. "You know it's against the rules to swim in anything but your regulation suits."

"But the cabin nine counselor lets her girls wear bikinis sometimes," Erin argued.

"Well, that's her business," Carolyn said firmly. "Cabin six follows the rules." She stopped in front of their cabin. "You girls go in and clean up. I'll go over to the office and pick up the mail."

3

The girls ambled into the cabin. "Carolyn can be a real pain sometimes," Erin complained. "She's such a stickler for rules. I can't believe she won't let me wear my bikini." She grabbed a brush from her nightstand, knocking a bottle of nail polish to the floor. Ignoring the polish, she sat down on her bed and began brushing her hair.

"I wore a bikini once," Megan said, and started giggling. "It was so embarrassing. I jumped into the pool and the top fell off."

"That's because you had nothing to hold it up with," Katie said, grinning. She took her night-gown off the bed and tossed it on the floor. Then she looked down at her own chest and sighed. "I don't think I could handle it either."

Erin continued to grumble as she tossed her bedspread over her wrinkled sheets. "Honestly, I don't think there's another counselor at Sunny-side who's as strict as she is."

"I don't know if that's true," Trina said, as she carefully smoothed her sheets. "And you have to admit, Carolyn's been pretty nice to us all summer."

Megan pulled some dirty clothes off her bed and shoved them into a drawer. "Yeah, but lately she hasn't been so great."

"She certainly has been criticizing us a lot," Katie said. She stood there holding her Walkman

4

and looking around for a place to stash it. Her nightstand was overflowing with junk, so finally she shoved it under her bed.

"I wish we had a counselor like the one in cabin nine." Erin sighed. "Those girls can get away with anything."

"Carolyn's let us get away with things," Trina said. "It's just lately she's been kind of . . . I don't know. Not as easygoing."

"Shh," Katie said, looking out the window. "She's coming."

"Did I get a package?" Megan asked as Carolyn entered. The counselor shook her head.

"The mail's not here yet. Are you guys ready for inspection?"

The girls took their places beside their beds. Carolyn slowly made her way around the room. Trina noticed with a sinking sensation that she didn't look very pleased.

She pulled back Erin's spread and frowned. "Erin, this bed is not made. And look at this nightstand! You were supposed to put all this stuff away!"

"What's the point?" Erin asked. "I'll just have to pull it all out again."

"Those are the rules," Carolyn said sternly. Then she looked at Sarah. "And what's all that under your bed?"

"Just books and stuff."

"Well, that's not where they're supposed to be." She touched the top of the bureau that Sarah and Megan shared and looked at her hand in disgust. "There's dust an inch thick here!" Then she opened Megan's drawer and eyed the jumble of clothes crammed inside. "Megan, this is a mess!"

"Sorry," Megan said meekly, but Carolyn just shook her head in annoyance. As she moved around the room, she had more and more criticisms for each of them. Trina was the only one who was spared. She was just naturally neat.

Carolyn's expression got darker as she discovered the Walkman under Katie's bed and the nightgown on the floor. "This place is a disaster!" she exclaimed. "You girls are getting sloppier and sloppier."

Trina couldn't blame her for being angry. Cabin six really was a mess, and Carolyn had been scolding them about this for ages. But she wasn't prepared for Carolyn's next words.

"I've been warning you every day for the past week. Well, you've had enough warnings. You're all going to stay here and really straighten up this place. Right now."

"But it's almost time for swimming," Katie protested.

"You'll have to miss it today. I'll go tell Darrell

6

you won't be coming. And when I come back, this cabin better be spotless!"

With that, she marched out of the cabin. The girls looked at each other in dismay. "It's so hot," Megan wailed. "I can't believe we're going to miss swimming!"

"Wow, she really is getting strict," Sarah moaned.

"See?" Erin said. "What did I tell you?"

Katie looked positively furious. "It's not fair!"

Trina had to agree. At least, it wasn't fair in *her* case. Her bed was perfectly made, and all her things had been neatly put away. Why should she have to be punished because the others were sloppy?

But there was nothing they could do about it. Everyone got to work straightening up the cabin. Trina helped Megan make her bed. The complaints flew across the room as they all scurried about.

"I'll bet they never make their beds in cabin nine," Erin muttered.

"This is worse than being at home," Sarah said. She crawled under her bed to gather her books. "Who does she think she is? Our mother?"

"My mother never looks under my bed," Megan grumbled.

7

"Neither does mine," Katie told her. "She says she's afraid of what she might find."

"I don't even have to make my bed at home," Erin announced. "We have a maid."

"Oh, quit griping," Trina said as she folded the clothes in Megan's drawer. "I'm the one who should complain."

"Yeah, you're right," Katie said. "You shouldn't be punished just because the rest of us are slobs."

"But that's not our fault," Megan said. "I mean, it's our fault that we're slobs. But that wasn't fair of Carolyn. She should have let Trina go to the pool."

"Cabin six sticks together," Trina remarked, with only a small sigh of regret. "C'mon, I'll help everyone."

It seemed to take ages to get the room in half-way decent shape. But they managed to finish by the time Carolyn returned. Once again, the girls stood by their beds as she made her inspection. To everyone's relief, she nodded. "This is the way it should look every day. Okay, you can go now."

"Go where?" Katie asked in a sullen voice. "It's too late to go to the pool for a swim, and it's not time for arts and crafts yet."

"The mail should be in by now," Carolyn said. "Why don't you go pick it up?"

It was better than doing nothing. The girls left

8

the cabin and headed toward the camp office. "You know what Brandy in cabin seven told me?" Megan said. "Their counselor has a tape player and tons of cassettes. She lets them play music as loud as they want, and they dance way past lights out."

"Carolyn would never let us get away with that," Katie said. "She's always making a big deal about how we have to get enough sleep."

"Now, be fair," Trina said. "She's right. If we didn't get enough sleep, we'd be tired all day."

"I don't want to be fair," Katie replied. "She's not fair to us."

Trina shook her head wearily. There was no point arguing with Katie when she'd made up her mind about something. It wouldn't do any good to remind her that they'd all been perfectly happy with Carolyn that summer. Until now.

As they approached the office, Sarah suddenly asked, "What's a CIT?"

"A what?" Trina asked.

Sarah pointed to a sign on the bulletin board outside the office. " 'CIT meeting,' " Trina read. She went up closer to read the rest of the announcement. Under the heading, the notice read,

If you're interested in becoming a counselor-in-training, come to a meeting in the main

9

office Tuesday at 3:00. Any girls twelve and older may apply.

Katie joined her. "Remember three years ago? We had one of the older campers hanging around us during free period, teaching us games and stuff. She must have been a CIT."

"We should do that," Megan said.

"Yuck," Erin said. "Who wants to hang out with babies?" Then she cocked her head thoughtfully. "Of course, I'd be a great counselor. I'd let them do anything they wanted. Not like Carolyn."

"Well, you can't," Katie said. "You're not twelve yet."

"Trina is," Megan noted. "Trina, are you going to be a CIT?"

Trina thought about it. "I don't know. It's an awfully big responsibility."

"You'd be good," Katie said. "You've got a lot of patience."

In all modesty, Trina had to admit Katie was right. Still, the idea of being in charge of a cabin made her feel funny. What if she couldn't handle it? "Let's go get the mail," she said abruptly.

They went inside the office. "Hi, Ms. Donovan," Katie said. "Is there any mail for cabin six?"

"Just a minute," Ms. Winkle's assistant said, and turned to the stack of letters and boxes piled on a table. Brandy from cabin seven walked in while they were waiting. "Hi," she greeted the cabin six girls. "How come you guys aren't at the pool?"

"Carolyn made us miss swimming because our cabin was a mess," Trina told her.

"You're kidding!" Brandy exclaimed. "Our counselor would never do anything like that to us."

"See what I mean?" Erin declared to the group. "None of the other counselors are as strict as Carolyn."

"What are you doing here?" Trina asked.

"I want to find out more about this CIT thing. I'm thinking about applying."

"Here you go," Ms. Donovan said. "There's a letter for your counselor. And there's this." *This* was a big cardboard box, addressed to Megan.

"Yay!" Megan exclaimed. "My mom told me this was coming when I talked to her on the phone last week."

"What is it?" Sarah asked.

"Goodies! My mother goes on a baking binge every now and then. There's going to be a cake in here and brownies and chocolate chip cookies. I'll bet there's peanut butter and crackers and Marshmallow Fluff, too. And barbecue flavored potato chips."

11

"Oh, Megan!" Sarah cried in ecstasy.

Brandy eyed the box in envy. "Lucky you."

"There's going to be more in here than we can eat," Megan said. She glanced to make sure Ms. Donovan wasn't listening and lowered her voice. "We should have a midnight feast. Hey, Brandy, why don't you bring your cabin over tonight and we'll have a party!"

"Wait a minute, Megan," Trina said. "We can't do that. Not that we don't want you guys," she added hastily to Brandy. "But no matter how quiet we are, Carolyn's bound to hear us."

"You're right," Katie said. "And with the mood she's been in lately, we'll get in serious trouble."

"Why don't you guys bring the box to our cabin?" Brandy suggested. "Could you sneak out without her hearing you?"

Katie considered this. "Probably. But won't your counselor get mad?"

Brandy giggled. "She wears these little plugs in her ears when she goes to bed. Once she falls asleep, an earthquake wouldn't wake her."

Trina was troubled. "I don't know. Like Katie said, we can't afford to get into any more trouble."

"But we won't," Katie said. "She won't even know about it."

"Oh, c'mon," Sarah urged. "It'll be fun!"

"We can play tapes and dance and eat," Brandy said.

"Sounds good to me," Erin said. Megan and Katie nodded with enthusiasm.

"I don't think it's a great idea," Trina began, but Katie pulled her aside and whispered in her ear.

"Trina, don't be a goody-goody. If you don't do it, no one will. And we haven't done anything fun like this in ages!"

Trina looked around. The eyes of all her cabin mates were on her. She couldn't spoil their fun. "Oh, all right." And she tried very hard to keep the reluctance she was feeling out of her voice.

There was only a glimmer of moonlight shining into the cabin. It was so dark that Trina had to grope for her shoes on the floor. And it was so quiet that she thought she could actually hear her heart thumping.

All around the room, the girls were silently pulling on their clothes. Katie crept over to the closed door leading to Carolyn's room, and pressed her ear against it. She stood there for a minute, listening. Then she beckoned to the others.

Without a word, they all got up. As Sarah opened the screen door, it squeaked slightly and they all stiffened. But there wasn't a sound from

Carolyn's room, so they proceeded out. Sarah held the door for Megan, who was carrying the box from home. When they were all out, she closed the door carefully.

Outside, there was a little more light from the moon. Katie put her finger to her lips, and they tiptoed past Carolyn's open window. Trina glanced at Megan worriedly. The little redhead had a tendency to giggle at times like this. But for once, she was able to control herself.

They hurried next door to cabin seven. Brandy stood at the door, waiting for them. "Hi!" she called out.

"Shh!" Trina hissed.

Brandy laughed. "It's okay. Like I said, we can make as much noise as we want. We just have to keep the lights off in case anyone comes by."

Trina couldn't believe it. Inside cabin seven, the girls were all talking in normal voices. A cassette player stood on a bureau, and while the music wasn't blasting, it was definitely loud enough to hear.

"This is fantastic!" Erin exclaimed.

"Are you sure your counselor can't hear this?" Trina asked in wonderment.

"Absolutely," one of the girls said. "We do this all the time!"

"You guys are so lucky!" Katie marveled.

14

"What's in the box?" a girl asked.

"Don't know for sure," Megan said. "But it's bound to be good. Anyone got scissors?"

They knelt on the floor around the box. Megan cut the string and tape. The first thing she pulled out was a big foil-wrapped square. She peeked under the wrapping. "Carrot cake," she announced.

"My favorite!" Sarah squealed.

Next came a covered pie tin. Megan pulled off the top and sniffed appreciatively. "Brownies!"

"With nuts?" Brandy asked.

Megan peered at them closely. "Yep! And chocolate frosting."

A general sigh of delight passed through the cabin. The sighs continued and increased with each item Megan drew out. "Cookies ... chips ... mmm, pecan squares. Crackers, peanut butter—"

"Chunky?" Katie asked.

"I can't see the label." Megan tried to turn the lid. "I can't get it off."

"Here," a cabin seven girl said, handing her the scissors. "Beat the side with this."

Megan began hitting the lid with the scissors. With each bang, Trina glanced anxiously at the door leading to the counselor's room. But Brandy was right. There wasn't a sound coming from there.

Finally, all the food was laid out on the floor.

15

"This is radical," Sarah murmured. "I don't know what to eat first."

But she didn't have to make that decision. Just as they were all reaching for one goody or another, the cabin door opened. Everyone froze. And the tiny glimmer of moonlight was all Trina needed to see the angry expression on Carolyn's face.

"What do you think you're doing!"

There was no need for anyone to answer that.

Within seconds, the food was repacked, and a woebegone group of girls followed Carolyn back to cabin six. Once inside, Carolyn faced them with her hands on her hips. "I can't believe this," she fumed. "I woke up in the middle of the night to get some water. And how do you think I felt when I saw you were all missing?"

The guilty campers stared at the floor. Finally, a miserable Trina raised her head. "I guess you were worried."

"That's putting it mildly! You girls are impossible! I don't know what I'm going to do with you!"

Now everyone was looking at her in surprise. They knew she'd be angry if she discovered them. But she sounded really upset.

Carolyn sighed deeply. "All right, we'll discuss this in the morning. Now go to bed."

Megan put the box down on the floor. As she did,

something fell out of her pocket. "Oh, Carolyn, this is for you." She handed her the envelope.

"When did this come?"

"This morning. I forgot to give it to you."

Carolyn looked like she was about to explode. "Megan! This could be something important!"

"Sorry," Megan whispered.

Carolyn glared at her. Then she shook her head wearily. "Just—just go to bed." She went into her room and shut the door.

"Wow," Katie murmured. "I didn't think she'd get *this* mad."

"Neither did I," Trina whispered. And as she crawled into bed, she couldn't help thinking that Carolyn really wasn't being like herself. Sure, they'd gotten into trouble before, and Carolyn had scolded them. But not like this. Trina had never seen her act this way before.

Something else must be bothering her, she thought. But what they had done certainly hadn't improved their counselor's mood. And she wished she could fall asleep right away, so she wouldn't have to feel so bad.

Chapter 2

In the dining hall the next morning, there was the usual noisy commotion going on. But the cabin six table was quiet. Silently, they all ate their breakfasts. Every now and then Trina glanced furtively at Carolyn. Their counselor barely touched her food. Her mouth was set in a tight line, and she was staring ahead at nothing in particular.

Trina tried to think of something to say. "These pancakes are good."

Carolyn's eyes focused on them. "Megan, stop playing with your food."

Startled, Megan looked up. "Huh?"

"Eat your breakfast," Carolyn commanded.

Next to Trina, Katie shifted uncomfortably in her seat, and finally spoke with forced cheerfulness. "I don't think it's going to be so hot today."

She looked at Carolyn expectantly, but all Car-

19

olyn responded with was, "Katie, don't talk with your mouth full. Sarah, take your elbow off the table."

Something's definitely wrong, Trina thought. She was on the verge of asking Carolyn if she was okay, but Carolyn's expression told her not to interfere. The counselor drummed her fingers on the table. Then, abruptly, she stood up. "I'm going to use the phone," she murmured, and walked away.

The girls stared after her with wide eyes. "Wow," Sarah said, "she must be really furious about last night."

"You don't think she's calling our parents, do you?" Megan asked.

"She wouldn't do that without telling us first," Katie said. "At least, I don't think she would. But she's been acting so creepy lately, who knows?"

"But she hasn't said a word about last night," Erin noted. "I thought we were going to get a big lecture this morning and a thousand demerits and no more trips to Pine Ridge."

"Maybe she forgot all about it," Megan piped up.

Katie gave her a scathing look. "Don't be ridiculous. I'll bet she just hasn't decided how we're going to be punished." She picked up her toast and chewed it thoughtfully. "That's why she's so quiet. She wants us good and scared."

"It's working." Trina sighed. "I'm definitely scared. She's acting awfully strange. We've done worse things than what we did last night. And she'd just scold us or give us a demerit or something." She shook her head worriedly. "This silent treatment is making me very nervous."

"Maybe it's got nothing to do with us," Sarah suggested. "Maybe she's not feeling well."

"But she'd tell us if she wasn't feeling well," Trina objected.

A light dawned in Erin's eyes. "I'll bet I know what's bugging her." The others turned to her.

"What?" Katie asked.

"She's got boyfriend problems," Erin stated.

"But she doesn't even have a boyfriend," Trina argued. "We'd know if she'd been seeing anyone. I don't think she's had a boyfriend since she broke up with Teddy."

Megan clapped a hand to her mouth. "Maybe that's her problem! Maybe she wants to get back with Teddy!" Her eyes searched the dining hall for the camp handyman, Carolyn's former boyfriend.

"Megan!" Sarah's expression was horrified. "Don't you dare even think about trying to get them back together!"

"Sarah's right," Trina said quickly. "Whatever's

bothering her, it's none of our business anyway. Unless it's us that's bothering her." She was glad to see Brandy from cabin seven ambling toward them. She needed a distraction.

"How many demerits did you get?" Brandy asked them.

"Don't know yet," Katie told her. "I'll bet your counselor doesn't even know about it."

"I just hope your counselor doesn't tell her," Brandy said. "This could ruin my chance to get accepted as a CIT."

"Are you going to that meeting this afternoon?" Trina asked.

Brandy nodded. "Any of you guys going?"

"Not me," Katie said. "I don't want to spend my last few weeks at camp baby-sitting."

"I think it could be fun," Megan said. "Playing at being a counselor."

Sarah shook her head in amusement. "Megan, you've got your head in the clouds so much you can barely take care of yourself. Forget about watching little kids."

Megan wasn't offended by Sarah's honest comment. "Yeah, you're right. Trina, you should do it. You'd be a great counselor."

There was no disagreement from the other girls at the table. "Yeah, come with me to the meeting," Brandy urged.

"I don't know," Trina said. "I have to think about it."

"Look," Sarah said. A line of young campers, seven or eight years old was walking past their table. "They're so cute."

"Why don't you apply?" Trina asked.

"Because you probably have to give up free period. And that's my only chance to read."

"The meeting's at three," Brandy said. "Try to come, okay?"

"Maybe," Trina replied. "Uh-oh, here comes Carolyn."

"I better get out of here," Brandy said. "See you guys later."

The girls watched with apprehension as Carolyn joined them at the table. She didn't look any happier than she had before.

Trina took a deep breath. She couldn't stand the suspense anymore. It was time to clear the air and find out what the cabin six girls were in for.

"Carolyn, we're sorry about last night."

Carolyn looked at them blankly. "What?"

"Sneaking out. We shouldn't have done it, and we're sorry. Right, guys?" The others nodded, their eyes firmly fixed on Carolyn.

"Well, don't do it again."

Trina stared at her in disbelief. Was that all she was going to say? No demerits, no losing privileges? She looked at the others. They all seemed stunned too.

But Carolyn was oblivious of their expressions. She was staring off into space again. And then she got up again. "I have to see Ms. Winkle. You girls can go on back and straighten up."

When she left, Katie looked at Trina in annoyance. "That was brilliant, reminding her about last night. Now she's probably asking Ms. Winkle what to do with us."

"I don't think so," Trina said. "I don't even think we're on her mind."

They got up, returned their trays, and headed back to the cabin. "How come you don't want to be a CIT?" Katie asked Trina as they walked.

"I didn't say I don't want to," Trina said. "I'm just not sure."

"But you like little kids," Katie remarked. "You told me, sometimes you baby-sit after school for the kids who live next door to you."

"That's true," Trina admitted. "And it's fun. I read them stories and teach them songs and games."

"You could do the same thing as a CIT."

"I know. But what if . . . what if they don't like me? What if they won't listen to me?"

"Of course they'll listen to you," Katie said with

spirit. "You'll be their counselor. They *have* to do what you say."

Megan had been listening to their conversation. "And they'll like you too. Why wouldn't they? Everyone likes you. You're a likable person."

"As long as you don't get all moody and strict like Carolyn's been," Erin warned her.

"Oh, I'd never be like that," Trina assured them. Back in the cabin, they all started making their beds.

"Everyone do a super-neat job," Trina said. "Maybe that will put Carolyn in a better mood."

"See?" Katie said, grinning. "You sound like a counselor already."

Trina grinned back. Maybe being a CIT *would* suit her.

"Maybe it's not a mood," Sarah said suddenly.

"What do you mean?" Trina asked.

"Maybe she's just changed. People do change, you know. She could be sick of us and sick of being a counselor."

Erin frowned. "Well, if she's going to be acting like this the rest of the summer, I wish she'd quit. Or maybe we could tell Ms. Winkle and get her fired."

Trina was shocked. "Erin! How can you say that? Carolyn's been a good friend to us."

"She's not being much of a friend now," Erin

pointed out. "If she goes on the way she is, do you want her to keep being our counselor?"

Trina didn't have an answer for that. "Come on, let's get this place cleaned up."

The girls worked quickly, and took extra pains to make sure the cabin was spotless. Sarah swept the floor, and Megan dusted the bureaus and nightstands. Even Erin got into the spirit, lining up all her cosmetics neatly on the nightstand.

"Here she comes!" Katie called, peering out the window. The girls hurried to their bunks, and stood there stiffly. When Carolyn walked in, Katie saluted her. "Cabin six, ready for inspection!"

Trina waited for Carolyn to smile, to show her approval at their unbelievably neat cabin. But Carolyn barely glanced at the room. "It's fine," she murmured. "You can go on to the pool."

She opened the door to her room. Trina stepped forward. "Um, Carolyn . . ."

"Yes?"

"Do you think I should apply to be a CIT?"

"If you want to," Carolyn said vaguely. She went into her room. Trina stared at the door closing behind her. She'd expected Carolyn to give her some advice, offer an opinion.

The others looked just as surprised. Katie spoke with clear disapproval. "That's not how a counselor is supposed to act."

"No, it isn't," Trina said. "When I'm a CIT, I'll always listen to my campers' problems." And with those words, she knew she'd made a decision.

At five minutes to three, Trina stood in front of the main office. Now that she was actually here, she wasn't so sure about her decision. She'd seen three girls go in already, and they were all older. They looked confident, as if they knew exactly what they were getting into.

Then she saw Brandy running toward her. "Oh good, I'm glad you're doing it too, Trina. C'mon, we don't want to be late." Well, she'd look foolish if she backed out now. So together the girls went into the office.

"We're here to apply for the CIT jobs," Brandy told Ms. Donovan.

"Go right on into Ms. Winkle's office," she instructed them. They did as they were told. The three older girls were already there, sitting on the couch. Brandy and Trina took the two remaining chairs.

The camp director beamed at them. "My, it's nice to have so many applicants! I wish we could use you all. But we only need three CITs, for cabins one, two, and three."

Trina wasn't sure if she felt relieved or disap-

27

pointed to hear this. Surely, Ms. Winkle would choose the older girls.

"First, I'm going to tell you what the job involves," Ms. Winkle continued. "Then, I'll interview each of you separately. I'll make a decision, and post the names of the chosen girls on the bulletin board outside at five o'clock."

The girls all nodded to show they understood, and Ms. Winkle went on. "The CITs will spend one hour a day, during free period, with an assigned cabin. It will be your responsibility to supervise the campers in an activity."

"What kind of activity?" one of the girls asked.

"That's up to you and your campers," Ms. Winkle said. "It can be an outdoor activity, such as an organized game, or you can use the activity hall for an indoor program."

"Will the regular counselor be with us?" Brandy asked.

"Yes, but only as an observer. *You* will be the official counselor during this period. Now, this isn't something to be taken lightly. You must be willing to commit yourself, to give up your free period, and you must have creative ideas. This isn't baby-sitting. Now, do you all want to be interviewed?"

Trina nodded along with the others, even though she knew she didn't have a chance.

"Fine," Ms. Winkle said. She looked them over. "Trina, I'll interview you first. The rest of you can wait outside."

Trina gulped as the other girls left the room. She had hoped Brandy would go before her, so she could tell Trina what to expect. But maybe this wasn't so bad. At least she'd get it over with.

"Now, Trina. Why do you think you'd be a good CIT?"

Trina tried to remember what her cabin mates had told her. "Well, I'm patient with people. I don't lose my temper easily. Back home, I baby-sit sometimes. And . . . and I've been coming here for three years. I know how counselors should act."

"And how is that?"

"I think a good counselor listens to her campers and helps them with their problems. And . . . and she shouldn't act one way sometimes and another way other times."

Ms. Winkle seemed to approve of that. "You're saying a counselor should be consistent in her behavior with campers. That's absolutely right. Campers should know what to expect from their counselors. Now, what kind of activities would you do with your cabin?"

Trina considered this. "I like reading out loud. And I could teach them songs and folk dances. I'm pretty good at that." She could feel her face redden as she said this. She'd never been the type to brag about herself.

But Ms. Winkle looked pleased. "All right, Trina, I think you've told me enough. You can go now, and send Brandy in."

"Thank you," Trina said and left. In the outer room, Brandy looked at her anxiously. "How was it?"

"Okay," Trina said. "I think. She wants to see you next."

"Meet me back here at five and we'll see if we made it," Brandy hissed before hurrying into Ms. Winkle's office. Trina had a feeling the older girls must have heard her. They were looking at Trina with sympathy—as if they already knew whose names would be on that list.

They were probably right, too. And as that thought entered her mind, something else did too. She realized that she really, really wanted to be chosen.

"Hey, Trina!" She turned and saw Katie and Megan running toward her. "Did you get the CIT job?" Megan asked.

"I won't know till five o'clock," Trina told them. "Ms. Winkle's going to post the names on the bulletin board."

"We'll come with you," Katie said. "Then we can celebrate if you get it."

Trina smiled, but she didn't say anything. She'd already decided she'd sneak away and check out the bulletin board by herself. If the news was bad, she'd just as soon not let the others see how she was feeling. After all, she was supposed to be the mature one in the group. And if she wasn't chosen to be a CIT, her reaction just might ruin her reputation.

Just after five, when no one was looking, Trina sneaked out of arts and crafts. Walking quickly, she made her way past the dining hall to the main office. As she got closer, she could see Brandy standing by the bulletin board. She squinted and tried to make out her expression. It looked like she was smiling.

Trina steeled herself to congratulate Brandy and shrug off any words of sympathy at *her*. But her preparations were unnecessary. As soon as Brandy saw her, she let out a squeal.

"We made it!"

Trina stopped short. "We?"

"We're both going to be CITs!"

Trina raced over to the bulletin board. Sure enough, there was the notice, and there were the names: Brandy, Trina, and Philippa, who must have been one of the older girls. Next to their

31

names was the cabin number they were assigned to. Trina had cabin three.

The girls threw their arms around each other and jumped up and down. "We start Thursday," Brandy said, pointing to the instructions on the notice. "Come on, let's go get some ice cream and celebrate!"

"Let's do that after dinner," Trina said. "It's just about rest period."

"Yeah, okay. It wouldn't look good for us to get into any trouble now!"

Trina agreed. "And I want to tell my cabin mates." They made plans to meet after dinner, and separated to go back to their own cabins.

Trina ran all the way. When she got to the cabin, she burst through the door. She was about to yell "guess what" when she realized that everyone was gathered on Megan's bed. And Carolyn was standing there, facing them.

"Oh, Trina, I'm glad you're back," Carolyn said. Her face was pale, and she wasn't smiling. "I've got something to tell you all."

Trina's excitement evaporated. This had to be it—their punishment for sneaking out. Silently, she joined the others on the bed.

"Girls, I'm going to have to leave Sunnyside for a while. You see, my mother's been ill, and I've been worried about her."

So that was why she'd been in such a bad mood, Trina thought.

"Anyway," she continued, "the letter I got the other day was from my brother, telling me that she needs an operation."

"Oh no," Sarah breathed. "Is it serious?"

"We don't know yet. But I've decided to go home, to help take care of her when she comes out of the hospital."

"How long will you be gone?" Katie asked.

"Just for a little while. Maybe two weeks, maybe less. It all depends. . . ." Her voice trailed off.

Trina felt pangs of sympathy for her. As usual, Erin was only thinking of herself.

"Who's going to be our counselor?" she asked.

"Ms. Winkle is talking to someone in Pine Ridge, and a substitute counselor will be coming on Thursday, the day I'm leaving. I don't know anything about her, but I'm sure she'll be just fine." She looked at her watch. "I'm going to the office to call my mother and let her know I'm coming." She started toward the door, and then stopped. "Oh, Trina, did you apply for the CIT job?"

"Yes," Trina said. "And I got it."

"All right!" Megan whooped, and then clapped a hand to her mouth. "Sorry, Carolyn."

"That's all right. I'm happy for her too. Congratulations, Trina. I know you'll do a fantastic job."

"Thanks," Trina said. "I hope so."

Everyone was quiet till Carolyn left the cabin. Then everyone started talking at once.

"Poor Carolyn," Sarah said. "So that's why she's been so grouchy."

"Yeah," Katie said. "I wish she'd told us before. Then we wouldn't have been complaining so much. Trina, what did Ms. Winkle ask you in the interview? Which cabin do you have?"

"A new counselor, yuck," Megan muttered. "Not you, Trina," she added hastily. "I was thinking about the new girl coming here."

"It could be great," Erin remarked. "I mean, I'm sorry about Carolyn's mother and all that. But even when Carolyn's in a good mood, she's stricter than a lot of other counselors."

"Maybe this new one will be more easygoing," Sarah said.

Trina heard all the conversation going on around her, but she wasn't really listening. A jumble of feelings were bouncing around inside her. Sympathy for Carolyn. Curiosity about the substitute who'd be coming. And her own new job, just two days away.

As everyone else chattered, she just kept hear-

34

ing the word "counselor." She wasn't even sure who they were talking about—Carolyn, the new girl, or herself. Trina Sandburg, counselor-in-training.

Chapter 3

Two days later, after breakfast, the girls walked with Carolyn down to the main road. "Can I carry your suitcase?" Trina asked.

"No thanks, it's not heavy."

"How are you getting home?" Megan asked.

Carolyn placed the suitcase down by the side of the road. "Teddy's driving me into Pine Ridge, and I can take a bus from there."

Everyone stood around awkwardly. "I hope your mother's okay," Sarah said.

"Thanks. I do too." Carolyn's eyes swept the group. "I know I've been a little hard on you guys lately. But believe it or not, I'm going to miss you."

"We'll miss you too," Katie responded. "It'll be weird having someone different in the cabin."

"I'm sure the new counselor will be very nice,"

Carolyn assured her. She smiled as she added, "As long as you're nice to her."

Megan looked at her with innocent eyes. "But, Carolyn, we're always nice!"

"Right," Carolyn said dryly. "Seriously, kids, this girl is new at camp counseling, so don't give her a hard time. No midnight feasts, okay?"

"No midnight feasts, we promise," Trina said. A car with the Camp Sunnyside symbol on it pulled up, and Teddy, the camp handyman, leaped out.

"Ready to go?" he asked, grabbing her suitcase.

"All ready," Carolyn replied. She turned to the girls. "Well, I'll see you all soon." She blew them all a kiss, and got into the car.

The girls watched silently as the car pulled away. "I *will* miss her," Katie said. "But I'm not really sorry she'll be gone for a while."

"Katie!" Trina exclaimed.

"I know what Katie means," Megan said. "I'm ready for a change."

"When is the new counselor coming?" Sarah asked.

"She's supposed to be here when we get back from the pool," Erin replied.

"We better hurry if we're going to get to the pool on time," Trina noted. They ran back up the slope to the cabin.

38

"I'm glad all you promised Carolyn was no midnight feasts," Katie told Trina as they changed into their bathing suits.

"What do you mean?" Trina asked. She noticed with alarm a familiar expression on Katie's face.

"We could have some fun with a new counselor!"

Megan's face lit up. "Ooh, you mean tricks and stuff like that?"

"Katie!" Trina eyed her best friend sternly. "You're not already planning pranks, are you?"

Katie grinned. "Nothing major. Actually, I haven't thought of anything—*yet.* But you heard Carolyn. This new girl's never been a counselor before. She won't know anything."

Megan giggled. "Yeah, we could definitely have some fun with her."

"At least, we'll be able to get away with some stuff," Erin said. She looked in the mirror and made a face. "Like, she might not know about the regulation bathing suits."

Trina gazed at them uneasily. She wasn't really worried about what they'd do to the new counselor. They weren't the kind of girls who'd do anything really awful. But something else was bothering her. What if her little campers were thinking this way about *her* right now?

39

"What's the matter?" Sarah asked her as they left the cabin and headed toward the pool.

"Oh, I was just thinking about this afternoon. I have my first free period with cabin three."

"Are you worried about *that?*" Erin asked, her words dripping with scorn. "For crying out loud, Trina, they're only nine years old. What can they do?"

Katie laughed. "No telling! Think of some of the things we did our first summer at camp."

Trina tried to remember. "Like what?"

Sarah grinned. "We almost drove Nina crazy! Like that first day, when Megan hid under the bed. Nina went running all over the place looking for her."

"And when she came back, I was sitting on my bed and I told her I'd been there all the time," Megan finished.

It all came back to Trina. Very clearly, in her mind, she saw the confusion on their counselor's face. "Let's not pull any stunts like that on the new counselor, okay?"

But no one was listening. They had reached the pool, and it was free swim day. Before she'd even finished speaking they were all jumping in. It was so hot, even Erin went in the water—but in the shallow end, so she wouldn't get her hair wet.

Trina sat on the edge and dangled her feet in

40

the water. Then she had an idea. She slid into the pool and swam over to where the others were gathered. "Listen, guys, I need to practice before this afternoon. Let's pretend I'm the counselor, and you're all a bunch of little kids."

Megan promptly stuck a thumb in her mouth, while Sarah puckered her lips and said, "Goo-goo."

"Not *that* little. Act like you're nine years old."

"Megan was probably still sucking her thumb when she was nine," Katie chortled.

Megan responded by slamming her hand into the water, causing a huge splash to hit Katie in the face.

"C'mon, get serious," Trina begged. "I need help." The urgency in her voice must have reached them, because they calmed down.

"What do you want us to do?" Katie asked.

"Um, let me think. First, we should go over to the shallow end." She was pleased to see her cabin mates follow her direction. Once they were all able to stand with their heads above water, they turned to her for the next instruction.

Trina smiled sweetly at them. "Very good, girls! Today, we're going to play a water game. Does anyone have a special game she'd like to play?"

Katie responded in an equally sweet voice. "Can we play 'drown the counselor-in-training'?"

Trina rolled her eyes. "Don't tease me. How about a game of water tag?"

"Goody goody," Megan squeaked.

"Now, who wants to be it?"

Katie's eyes searched the pool and lit on Erin. Their cabin mate had her elbows up on the ledge, her face turned to the sun. Her legs went up and down in lazy kicks, and she appeared to be completely oblivious of their conversation.

Sarah made a babyish pouting face. "I don't think Erin wants to play with us."

Trina tried to envision this as a real situation. "Maybe she's just shy. Why don't you ask her nicely if she'd like to play?"

"I've got a better idea," Katie stated. "The first girl to duck Erin under and get her hair wet wins!" Before Trina could say anything, Katie, Megan, and Sarah all charged Erin, who shrieked as they dragged her away from the ledge.

"Girls! Girls! Stop that!" Trina yelled. But no one paid any attention to her. Glumly, she watched as they dunked a furious Erin.

Well, what could she expect from them, she told herself. They weren't going to take orders from her, not even make-believe ones. But it would be different that afternoon with the nine year olds. They'd *have* to listen to her. After all, she'd be their counselor, and campers paid attention to their counselors.

At least, they *usually* did.

Despite the heat, the girls had a race back to the cabin. Trina had so much nervous energy she ran even faster than usual, sprinting ahead of Katie just as they reached the cabin. "I win!" she yelled as she burst inside. And then she stopped short.

An older girl, with pale brown hair, was sitting on a bed looking a little bewildered. When she saw Trina, she quickly rose and smoothed the folds of her flowered dress. Then she offered a thin smile. "Hello."

Behind Trina, the other campers gathered. "Are you the new counselor?" Katie demanded.

"Yes. My name is Lucy Meadows." She was twisting her hands as she spoke. Trina couldn't blame her for being nervous, the way they were all staring at her. She stepped forward and held out her hand. "I'm Trina."

Lucy took her hand and then quickly withdrew it. "You're wet."

"Well, we've just been swimming," Trina explained, though she thought that should be obvious from the fact that they were wearing bathing suits and their hair was dripping.

43

"Oh, of course." A high-pitched giggle escaped the new counselor's lips. "How silly of me."

Since the others were still staring, Trina went ahead and introduced them. "That's Katie, Megan, Sarah, and Erin."

"Golly," Lucy said, "how am I going to remember all your names?"

"There are only five of us," Katie pointed out. "Can't you remember five names?"

Trina frowned at Katie's rudeness. "Don't worry," she told Lucy, "if you forget our names, we'll remind you."

"Thank you," Lucy said. "You know, I've never been a counselor before. In fact, I've never even been to a camp." Once again, she giggled.

Trina could see Katie's lips twitch as if she were trying to hold back a laugh. She shot her a warning look and turned back to Lucy. "Did Ms. Winkle tell you what you're supposed to do?"

Lucy nodded. "She said I should go with you to all your activities today, so I can learn my way around." She went over to the bulletin board by the door and looked at the schedule. "I guess we're supposed to go to archery now."

Erin spoke up. "Would it be all right if we took a shower and changed first?"

Trina flinched at the sarcasm in her voice. But Lucy didn't seem to notice it. "Oh, how silly of me!

44

Sure you can." And she punctuated that with another awful giggle. Then she sat back down on a bed. "I'll just wait right here for you, okay?"

The girls hurried into the bathroom and turned on the water full blast so they could talk without being heard by the counselor.

"She's a nerd," Katie stated flatly.

"That giggle's going to get on my nerves," Sarah said.

"If I had hair like that, I'd wear a wig," was Erin's comment.

"C'mon, you guys, give her a chance," Trina urged. "You can't blame her for being nervous." But she made a mental note not to let her own feelings show when she found herself in the same position.

"Why did you decide to become a counselor?" she asked Lucy as they walked to the archery range.

"I just thought it would be fun to be with children," Lucy said. "I've always liked baby-sitting."

"We're not exactly babies," Katie said.

"We're almost not even children anymore," Erin added.

Lucy giggled.

"Hey, look what I found?" Megan, who had been lagging behind, ran toward them with her hands

45

cupped. She opened them to reveal a small grass lizard.

"How cute," Trina remarked.

"What is it?" Lucy asked. She came forward and looked into Megan's hands. Then she shrieked.

"Ick! That's horrible!" She backed away as if the tiny lizard was a boa constrictor.

"It's just a baby lizard," Megan said. "It won't hurt you."

Lucy was pale. "I don't care! I just can't stand creepy, crawly things."

Katie spoke in her usual blunt way. "Then I don't think you're going to like it very much here. This place is full of creepy, crawly things."

Lucy looked around fearfully as if she expected a thousand creepy, crawly things to jump out at her. "What a wimp," Katie murmured.

"Shh," Trina said. "Megan, why don't you put that lizard back where you found it."

"But I wanted to keep it in our cabin."

Lucy's face went from pale to white. "Oh, no! Not in the cabin! It might crawl in my bed!"

Even Trina had a hard time hiding a smile. Reluctantly, Megan placed the lizard down gently by the side of the path, and the girls continued on to the archery range. As they picked up their bows and arrows, Lucy watched them with her mouth slightly open. "Those are real arrows!"

"Well, of course they are," Erin said. "What did you expect?"

"But that's so dangerous! Children shouldn't be playing with real arrows!"

"It's only dangerous if you point them in the wrong direction," Katie replied. Casually, she began stringing her bow while facing Lucy. Lucy's eyes darted around as if she were seeking a place to hide.

As much as Trina felt sorry for the new counselor, she had to admit Katie was right. This girl was a major wimp. And as she began to string her own bow, she felt some relief thinking that the girls in cabin three couldn't possibly say that about *her.*

Trina marched across the path to cabin three, hoping she looked a lot more confident than she felt. She was pleased to see a counselor sitting on the steps of the cabin.

"Hi. You must be Trina," the girl said. "I'm Karen." She cocked her thumb at the cabin. "The girls are having their rest period, but they'll be up in a minute. Then they're all yours."

Trina gulped. All hers? Wasn't Karen planning to stay with them?

Apparently not. "I think it's a good idea for you to be alone with them," Karen continued. "Oth-

47

erwise, they'll just turn to me for direction and ignore you."

"What should I do with them?" Trina asked.

"Anything you like. They've been outdoors all day. Why don't you take them to the activities hall?"

"Okay." Trina liked the idea of keeping them indoors. It would be easier to keep an eye on them.

Karen checked her watch. "Come on in, and I'll introduce you." Trina followed her inside, a fixed smile already planted on her face.

"Girls, this is your new counselor-in-training, Trina."

"Hi," Trina said. She was horrified to hear that one word come out almost as squeaky as Lucy's had. And she didn't like the fact that the six faces looking at her weren't smiling.

"Why don't you introduce yourselves," Karen suggested.

Names flew by—Lisa, Amber, Casey . . . Trina was trying so hard to fix the right name to the right face that she missed half the names she heard.

"Okay, Trina, take over," Karen said. "Just bring them over to arts and crafts when you're done." And she left the cabin. Trina took a deep breath.

"I'm very happy to know you all," she began, but one little girl interrupted. "Why?"

"Well, because, because, I just am," Trina said lamely. "I'd like to take you over to the activities hall."

"What are we going to do there?" a girl asked. Trina couldn't remember if she was Amber or Lisa.

"I'm going to teach you a folk dance." She winced as a resounding groan filled the room. "Uh, would you rather learn a song? Or hear a story?"

They didn't look any more enthusiastic about those suggestions than they did about the folk dance. Trina swallowed. "Well, let's just go over there and we'll decide."

She breathed a sigh of relief as the girls got off their beds. As they walked to the activities hall, the girls whispered among themselves and basically ignored Trina.

I have to get them talking to me, Trina thought. She turned to the closest girl. "Is this your first year at Sunnyside, Casey?"

The small fair-haired girl gave her a look of disdain. "I'm Courtney."

"Oh, I'm sorry. Courtney. Is this your first year?"

"Yeah." Then she turned away, whispered

something to the girl walking next to her, and they both started giggling.

Trina tried another girl. "You're Amber, right?"

"No, I'm Lisa."

"Lisa," Trina repeated. She could have sworn the freckled redhead was Amber. "Do you like folk dancing, Lisa?" A chorus of giggles followed this question.

"I hate it."

"Oh." Trina forced a bright smile. "Well, maybe you'll like this one."

In the music room at the activities hall, Trina selected a record. The girls watched silently as she placed it on the record player. "This dance is called the Virginia reel. Has anyone ever done it before?"

There was no response. "I'll show you the first step. But I'll need a partner. Who'd like to be my partner?" She expected a flurry of hands to go up. None did. Trina's smile faded a bit, but with effort she pulled it back. Turning to the small fair-haired girl, she asked, "How about you, Courtney?"

"I'm Casey." There was another chorus of giggles. Trina could have sworn that one had said her name was Courtney. But she could be wrong. "Okay, Casey. Will you be my partner and help me show this step?"

Looking like she'd rather jump off a cliff, Casey

joined her. "First we join hands. Then you step forward with your right foot."

Casey immediately stepped forward with her left. "No, your right foot." Casey switched feet. "Okay, now bring your other foot together with this one."

"Huh?"

"Like this." Trina demonstrated. "Are the rest of you watching?"

They didn't bother to respond, and it wasn't necessary. The others were huddled in a group, whispering and giggling. This wasn't working.

"Maybe we should all do this together," Trina said. She started pairing them up. Tapping the redhead on the shoulder, she said "Lisa, you stand with—"

"I'm Courtney."

Trina frowned. "Well, whatever your name is, stand with—what's your name?"

The pigtailed girl seemed to take her time considering this question. "Marsha."

Trina didn't even remember a Marsha being introduced. "Okay, Courtney with Marsha. Casey with Amber—"

"I'm Lisa."

"And I'm Amber," another girl said.

Trina was totally confused. "Just—pair up, okay?" When she had her three groups of two girls

51

each, she put the needle on the record. The music started. "Now, everyone take a step forward."

They did as they were told, and she called out, "Now step to the left." Half of them stepped to the left, the others to the right, and they all bumped into each other. "No, no!" Trina exclaimed, but no one was listening. They were all snickering.

"Courtney, don't take such big steps!"

"I'm Amber."

Trina stared at her. Was she losing her mind? As the snickers expanded to hysterical giggles, the truth dawned on her. They were all changing their names. Well, she'd straighten it all out later.

"Come on, you guys," she pleaded. "Don't you want to learn this dance? Now listen to my directions."

But they wouldn't. When she told them to move to the left, they'd move to the right. At first, she thought they simply didn't know left from right. But when she instructed them to step forward, and they all stepped backward, she realized they were doing this on purpose.

The hour couldn't pass quickly enough for Trina. They kept on giving different names, no one listened to her directions, and by the end of the period they didn't know any more about the Virginia reel than they had when they started.

And Trina was a nervous wreck. It was enormously difficult to keep her voice calm and even. "I guess you guys aren't into folk dances. Maybe tomorrow we'll do something different. Like—we'll learn a song."

The faces and groans that greeted this suggestion made it clear they were no more into singing than dancing. "Or something else," Trina added quickly. "It's time for you to go on to arts and crafts now."

They all started running toward the door. "Wait!" Trina yelled. "I'm supposed to take you!" She ran after them, but they didn't wait. As she tore out the door, she caught a glimpse of two older campers looking at her curiously. She must have looked like an idiot, chasing after a bunch of nine year olds.

The girls slowed down just as they reached the arts and crafts cabin, and Trina realized why. Karen, their counselor, was waiting for them in front of the building.

The campers stopped giggling, and greeted Karen cheerfully. As they went into the cabin, Trina called out, "See you tomorrow!" No one even looked back at her.

"How did it go?" Karen asked.

Trina hesitated. Karen looked sincerely interested. But Trina had too much pride to confess that the hour had been a total disaster. "Fine," she managed to say. Karen smiled, but her expression was skeptical.

"Really, it was fine," Trina insisted. "I'll see you tomorrow." And as she headed back to cabin six, she kept telling herself that tomorrow she would make it fine. If only she could figure out how.

Chapter 4

"I was stupid," Trina told her cabin mates that evening. They were all sitting on the steps in front of cabin six, watching the sun go down. "I fell for a trick we pulled on Nina three years ago."

"Which trick was that?" Sarah asked.

"The one where we all kept changing names to confuse the counselor."

"I remember that one!" Erin said. "We did it our first day. Whenever Nina called me Erin, I'd tell her my name was Katie. Then she'd call me Katie, and I'd say my name was Trina. It took Nina three days to figure out what we were doing!"

"At least it only took me an hour." Trina sighed. "But I felt like a real idiot."

"We never tried to pull that one on Carolyn, did we," Katie mused.

"It's too late now," Sarah said. "After two months, she knows us!"

"Should we try it on Lucy?" Erin wondered.

"Let's not," Trina said. "She's freaked out enough as it is. Where is she, anyway?"

"She's in her room with the door closed," Katie said. "And she's *knitting*. Can you believe it?"

"How do you know she's knitting if the door's closed?" Trina asked.

"Ooh, that's right, you were gone during free period," Sarah said. "Katie, tell her what you found."

"I discovered a tiny hole in the wall," Katie explained. "Only about a half-inch wide. But if you put your eye against it, you can see inside the counselor's room."

"Are you saying you've been spying on her?" Trina asked in a shocked voice.

"Sure, why not?" Katie asked. "Look, we've got to get rid of her. There's no way we can put up with Lucy the loser for two weeks."

"Trina, didn't you see her at the stables?" Erin asked. "She was so freaked out by the horses she wouldn't even help me saddle mine."

"She didn't want us to play soccer because she was afraid we'd hurt ourselves," Katie said.

"And she took away my book during free period," Sarah told her. "She said it was too *mature* for me."

"She wanted us to play a game," Katie added. "Are you ready for this? She wanted to play Simon Says! As if we were babies or something!"

"Ick," Trina said. "I guess she really doesn't know anything about being a camp counselor."

"We *have* to get rid of her," Katie said again. "Only I can't figure out a way."

"You'll come up with something," Sarah said. "I just wish you'd come up with an idea fast."

The girls in cabin three were probably talking about her right now, Trina thought. And maybe they were saying the same thing. She looked away from the girls. Megan was a few yards away, picking something up from the grass.

"Megan, what are you doing?" Trina called to her.

Megan ran over to them. "Look at these." She was carrying in her hands a bunch of tiny toads, no more than an inch long. She had her hands cupped to keep them from jumping out.

"What are you going to do with them?" Trina asked.

"I don't know. I've just been gathering them. I guess I'll let them go."

"Wait a minute," Katie said suddenly. "I just had a brilliant idea!" She picked up one of the

57

toads and examined it closely. "I'll bet we can squeeze these through the hole that goes into the counselor's room. And they'll land right on her bed!"

"Ohmigosh, she'll freak out!" Erin squealed. "You saw how scared she was of the little lizard. Can you imagine what she'll do when she sees these?"

"But that's so mean," Trina protested.

No one paid any attention to her objection. Megan poured the little toads into Katie's hands, and ran back into the grass for more.

Trina watched the procedure in dismay. There was no way she could stop them from doing this. Sarah and Erin were all for it too.

"We've got enough," Katie decided. "C'mon, let's go inside and do it."

Reluctantly, Trina followed them inside. She sat down on her bed and watched as Katie went to the wall that separated the main cabin from the counselor's room. She took a toad and squeezed it through the hole. Then she squeezed another and another.

She didn't have to use up all the toads. Just after she'd pushed the fifth one through, they heard a scream. Quickly, Katie tossed the remaining toads out the door. And then Lucy came running out.

"Help! Help!" she wailed.

Katie's face was the picture of innocence. "What's the matter?"

"There are disgusting little creatures on my bed!"

The girls ran into her room. Sarah picked up one of the toads. "You mean, these? They won't hurt you."

"Get them out of here!" Lucy shrieked. The girls scurried around the room looking for the baby toads.

"Did you get them all?" Lucy asked.

"Don't know," Erin said. "They're so tiny . . ."

Lucy's eyes were wide with fear. "I'm not sleeping here tonight! I'm not spending one more minute in this cabin!"

"But we have to have a counselor!" Trina exclaimed.

That fact didn't seem to concern Lucy. She grabbed her suitcase and tossed it on the bed. She opened a drawer, pulled out her clothes, and threw them in the suitcase. Then, suitcase in hand, she ran out of the room and out of the cabin.

The girls watched her departure in silent amazement. "Wow," Katie breathed. "I didn't think she was going to take it that hard."

"She's even wimpier than I thought she was," Sarah said.

59

Even Trina had to admit that Lucy wasn't exactly suited to being a counselor if a little prank like that was going to send her home. "I guess she's going to see Ms. Winkle."

"We won't get into any trouble," Katie said with assurance. "Lucy doesn't know how the toads got in there."

"But Ms. Winkle's not going to let us stay here without a counselor," Megan reminded her. "What do you think she's going to do?"

"She's not going to be able to find a counselor for tonight," Katie said. "Let's start a Monopoly game. We'll probably be able to stay up all night and play."

But that wasn't to be. Fifteen minutes later, Donna, the arts and crafts counselor, appeared at their door. "Hi!" Megan said. "What are you doing here?"

"I'm going to be staying with you girls tonight," Donna said.

"Did Lucy quit?" Trina asked.

"Yes. I'm afraid she wasn't cut out to be a camp counselor." Her eyes examined them suspiciously. "I don't suppose you girls had anything to do with that decision."

Megan muffled a giggle, and Donna sighed. "Well, she wouldn't have lasted long anyway, not if she was afraid of miniature toads."

60

"Are you going to be our counselor till Carolyn gets back?" Sarah asked eagerly. Everyone liked Donna.

But Donna shook her head. "No, just for a couple of nights. Ms. Winkle says she knows someone in Pine Ridge who can be here the day after tomorrow."

"I hope she's not a major dork like that Lucy," Erin said.

"I'm sure Ms. Winkle will question this one a little more thoroughly," Donna said. She shook her head ruefully. "I still can't believe that poor girl couldn't stick it out even one full day."

Neither could Trina. And there was one thing she knew for sure. No matter what kind of pranks cabin three pulled, they weren't going to get rid of *her* that easily.

Trina went over to cabin three a little earlier the next day, so she could have a talk with Karen first. By the time their conversation was finished, she felt sure she knew which girl was which. And when she stood before the girls in the cabin, she spoke briskly.

"Now, what would you like to do today? Something indoors or outdoors?"

The freckled redhead spoke. "Outdoors."

"Okay, Amber—"

"I'm Lisa."

Trina smiled kindly. "No you're not, you're Amber. Listen, you guys, remember that I'm a camper too. And my cabin mates have pulled every prank on a counselor you can think of."

She thought she sounded terribly self-confident. But she couldn't help shuddering slightly as she saw the younger girls exchange mischievous looks. She'd seen that expression on Katie's face. These girls had a plan—and she was going to have to watch them very closely.

She smiled brightly. "Okay, you want to do something outdoors. Any ideas?"

"We want to play tag," Amber stated, and the others nodded in agreement.

Trina wasn't crazy about the idea. Tag could get rough. But she really wanted them to like her. "Okay. Let's go outside."

She led them into the play area just outside the cabin. "Who wants to be it?"

"I'll be it," Amber announced, and no one made any objection to that. She started running, and the others went in pursuit.

"Stay in this area!" Trina yelled, but that didn't appear to be their intention. Amber started down the slope toward the road, and the others followed. Within seconds, they had disappeared from view over the ridge.

Trina had a terrible vision of Amber running out into the road. She chased after them. "Don't go that way! Come back here! Please!"

Amber was running along the side of the road. But as soon as Trina reached the bottom of the slope, Amber turned and started running back up toward the cabin. The others followed, though none of them looked particularly anxious to catch her.

Breathless, Trina went back up after them. For a moment, they all disappeared over the ridge, but she could hear them yelling. Then, suddenly, the area went silent. And Trina heard one lone voice yelling, "Help!"

She tore over the top of the slope. And when the girls came into view, she gasped.

They were gathered in a circle, looking down. Trina drew closer. In the middle of their circle, Amber lay on the ground, very still. "What happened?" Trina cried out.

"She fell!" one of the girls exclaimed. "She hit her head on a rock!"

Trina's heart thumped wildly. She bent down next to the motionless girl. She was lying facedown, but Trina could see a pool of blood lying next to her, and streaks of red dripping down the side of her head.

"I think she's dead," someone said solemnly.

63

Trina tried not to let the panic overwhelm her. "Get help," she snapped. "Go to the infirmary!" When no one moved, she turned her head from the body on the ground. "Why are you just standing there?"

And then one of them giggled. Another nudged her with an elbow, but it was too late. Trina let her breath out. She touched what she had thought was blood and sniffed it.

"Okay," she said in resignation. "Where's the ketchup bottle?"

"I can't believe I was so gullible," Trina moaned to her cabin mates after telling them the story at dinner. She'd waited till Donna left the table to talk to Ms. Winkle before reporting on her experience with cabin three. She didn't want to confess her stupidity in front of a real counselor. "I'm as bad as Lucy, falling for a stunt like that."

Katie patted her shoulder. "You're not as bad as Lucy. You didn't quit, did you?"

"No, but I'm thinking about it."

"It's not like you to give up so easily," Sarah said reprovingly.

"But they don't like me."

"No one likes counselors at first," Erin said.

"But they won't even listen to me!"

"Then make them listen," Megan said.

"How?"

No one had an answer for that. Trina saw Donna on her way back to the table. "Don't say anything about it in front of her, okay? I don't want Ms. Winkle to find out I'm having such a rough time."

Her friends nodded with understanding. "Well, your new counselor should be here first thing tomorrow morning," Donna announced.

"Do you know anything about her?" Katie asked.

Donna shook her head. "But Ms. Winkle said she's definitely not the type who will scare easily."

"Then we'll just have to try harder," Katie whispered to Trina. Trina couldn't even smile. She was feeling a lot more sympathy for counselors than she used to feel.

Chapter 5

Something woke Trina up early the next morning. It was a voice—an unfamiliar one. Donna, Trina thought sleepily. But no, Donna didn't have a loud, strident voice. She opened her eyes.

Donna was standing there, her hair tousled and a robe wrapped loosely over her pajamas. She looked sort of dazed, as if she was still half asleep. But the woman who was doing the talking was wide-awake.

Trina rubbed her eyes and hoisted herself on her elbow to get a better look at the stranger. The woman was very tall. She was wearing crisp-looking pants and a tailored shirt. Around her neck was a chain with a whistle attached.

"Why aren't the girls out of their beds?" she demanded.

"It's only seven o'clock," Donna explained. "They don't get up for another hour."

"That's ridiculous. If they went to sleep at a decent hour, they would all be up and about by now. I'll take care of that immediately." She put the whistle to her lips and blew.

The shrill screech filled the cabin. From every bed, a startled head rose.

Megan stared ahead blankly. "What's the matter?"

"Is it a fire?" Sarah asked.

"No, it's your new counselor." The woman strode to the center of the cabin. "My name is Miss Crawford. And I want every one of you up and dressed in five minutes."

No one moved. Not completely awake, they were all staring at her in stunned amazement. Miss Crawford checked her watch. "You now have four minutes and fifty-five seconds. I recommend that you *move*."

The tone in her voice brought forth an immediate response. The girls jumped out of their beds. Even Donna looked a little frightened. She scurried back into her room.

As they rapidly dressed, the girls exchanged wondering glances. But something about Miss Crawford's presence told them not to talk.

Donna emerged from her room, dressed. "I, uh, guess I'll go now that your new counselor is here."

Throwing the girls a weak smile, she fled the cabin.

Miss Crawford surveyed the campers. "Get ready for inspection," she ordered.

Katie stepped forward. "We have inspection after breakfast."

Miss Crawford fixed stern eyes on her. "From now on, you'll have inspections when I order them. Now, and after breakfast, and before dinner too." She ignored the horrified expressions on the campers' faces and walked down the center of the room, gazing at each of them with a look of disgust.

"You! What's your name?"

"Sarah."

"Where are your socks?"

"Uh, sometimes I don't wear them."

"Socks are regulation attire! Put them on immediately!" She moved on. "Who are you?"

"M-M-Megan."

"Your hair is a mess."

Megan's hand flew up to her mass of curls. "That's just the way it is."

"That's no excuse! Do something about it!"

For each girl she had a criticism. Katie's tee shirt was wrinkled, Trina's shoelace had a knot in it. Erin was ordered to remove her nail polish. When she'd finished with her inspection, she stood before them, arms folded and face grim. "This is the sorriest looking excuse for a cabin I've ever seen."

Trina wondered how many she'd seen before, but she didn't dare ask.

"You all look like a bunch of lazy good-for-nothings," she continued. "Well, that's going to end now. I plan to whip this cabin and you campers into shape."

Trina looked at Katie. She'd never before seen her best friend look so totally, utterly stunned.

"Eyes forward!" Miss Crawford snapped. Trina jerked her head back. "Now, according to this schedule, you're supposed to rise at eight o'clock, and lights out is at ten. Well, that's nonsense. From now on, lights out will be at nine, and you'll be up at seven."

Katie seemed to have recovered a bit. At least, she found her voice. "Why?"

"So you'll have time to do your calisthenics before breakfast."

"Calisthenics?" Sarah went pale.

"We get plenty of exercise," Erin pointed out.

"I sincerely doubt that," the counselor retorted. "Look at you. You're soft and flabby. And look at this cabin. It's a mess. The beds aren't even made."

"That's because we make them after breakfast," Trina said hesitantly.

70

"From now on you make them before breakfast," Miss Crawford replied. "You better understand right now, I run a tight ship. You follow my orders, and we'll all get along fine. Now, make those beds. *Now.*"

The girls ran to their beds and started making them. Miss Crawford walked around the cabin bellowing directions. "Smooth those sheets! Tuck those corners tighter!"

Climbing down from her top bunk, Katie muttered to Trina, "What does she think this is, the army?"

Suddenly, the counselor was standing there. "What did you say?"

The usually feisty Katie was speechless. "Uh, nothing."

"I'm glad to hear it. I will not tolerate any back talk. Now, everyone wash her hands."

Trina could see Erin's face turning red, and she knew why. They were all eleven or twelve years old. They didn't have to be told to wash their hands.

But they did as they were told. And as soon as the door to their washroom closed, they all started talking at once.

"She's unbelievable!" Katie gasped.

"She scares me," Megan whimpered.

Sarah nodded fervently. "Even Lucy would be better than her!"

"If she thinks she's going to boss me around," Erin fumed, but she didn't get to finish her threat. The door swung open. "There's too much chatter in here! Finish washing and come out for inspection."

"We just had inspection," Katie protested.

But this turned out to be a different inspection. Miss Crawford actually made them hold out their hands so she could see if they were clean enough. Then she ordered them outside.

"We will start off with jumping jacks," she announced. She blew her whistle. "Begin!"

She put them through a routine that was worse than Trina's phys. ed. class back at school. Marching back and forth in front of their line, she barked out her orders. When their ordeal was over, everyone was out of breath.

"Form a single line," she commanded. "We will now march to the dining hall."

Erin was right behind Trina. "This is humiliating!" she whispered. "What if someone sees us?"

"No talking in line!" Miss Crawford snapped. "You can talk at breakfast."

But no one did. How could they, with this drill sergeant sitting right there? So they ate in silence, afraid of even looking at one another for fear Miss Crawford might not like their expressions.

After breakfast, she marched them back to the cabin. And then they were put to work, dusting, sweeping, even cleaning the windowsills.

Finally, they were allowed to change into their bathing suits. But even then they weren't set free. Miss Crawford marched them to the swimming pool. For a moment, Trina was afraid she planned to stay there and observe their swimming lesson. But she just turned to Darrell and said, "Please report any infractions of rules to me." And she left.

Darrell grinned at the girls. "Looks like you've got a very serious counselor."

"No kidding," Katie moaned. "She's like a warden in a prison! Guys, what are we going to do?"

"You're the one with the brilliant ideas," Megan said. "Think of a way to get rid of her."

Sarah grimaced. "Can you imagine trying to pull a prank on *her?* She doesn't strike me as the type to get freaked out by baby toads."

"And I thought Carolyn was strict," Erin moaned. "This is terrible!"

"Wait, you guys, let's not get too upset yet," Trina said. "Maybe she's just coming on strong right now to keep us from pulling any stunts on

73

her. She'll probably loosen up when she realizes we're not so awful."

"You really think so?" Megan hopefully.

"Absolutely," Trina said, with a lot more confidence than she felt.

But that was not to be. Miss Crawford reappeared after their swimming session to march them back to the cabin. After they changed back into their shorts and shirts, they were marched to archery, then to arts and crafts. All the while, the woman never cracked a smile or made any conversation with them. All she did was bellow orders.

The minute they were left alone in arts and crafts, they huddled. "What are we going to do?" Megan moaned. "We can't live with her for two weeks!"

"Maybe we should try talking to her," Trina suggested. "Tell her how we usually do things."

"How can we talk to her?" Erin asked. "We're not even allowed to speak!"

"We have to give her a chance," Trina said. "It's not easy being a new counselor. She's only been here half a day."

"I don't think she's going to change," Sarah said. "Do you, Trina?"

"She might." Or she might not, Trina added silently. That was a depressing thought.

74

But then something else occurred to her. As mean and strict as Miss Crawford was, the girls *were* doing what they were told to do. And that gave her an idea.

She didn't know if she could pull it off. After all, she'd never been much of an actress, and what she had in mind certainly wasn't her style. But it was worth a shot.

As she headed to cabin three that afternoon, she fixed an image of Miss Crawford firmly in her head. And when she entered, she hoped the stern expression she could see in her mind was visible on her face.

The campers were still lying around on their beds. They didn't even look at her. Trina didn't have a whistle around her neck, but she could improvise. She put two fingers to her mouth and blew.

That got their attention. And before she could lose it, Trina spoke in a voice she'd never used before. "Everybody up! Now!"

She was taken aback by how ferocious she sounded—almost a perfect imitation of Miss Crawford's voice. And what was even more amazing was the way the girls responded. Exactly the way cabin six had.

For a second they were frozen. Trina repeated her command, only louder and harsher. This time she got action. The girls got off their beds, exchanging startled looks.

They stood there, gazing at her in wonderment as she walked down the center of the cabin. "This place is a mess! I see clothes and stuff on the floor. And your beds are rumpled."

"We've been lying on them," Courtney said. "That's why they're rumpled."

"Don't talk back to me! I want all these beds made over. Get everything off the floor and put it away. Then we'll have inspection."

"We already had inspection this morning," Casey protested. "Karen said we were okay."

"I don't care what Karen said," Trina stated. "I'm in charge during this period. And you have to do what I say! Now *move.*"

She held her breath. And to her amazement, they actually moved. They didn't look very happy about it, but they started picking stuff up off the floor and smoothing their beds.

"Form a line," Trina snapped. They did. Trina folded her arms across her chest and glared at them. At least, she hoped she was glaring. "From now on, I run a tight ship. You do what I say, or you're in serious trouble." She walked slowly down the line and paused in front of the redhead, Lisa. The little girl had her hair pulled back in a ponytail from which wisps of hair had escaped.

"Your hair is a mess. There's a smudge on your cheek. And your shirt is wrinkled. That's not how a Sunnyside girl should look."

Lisa's lower lip trembled, and for a second, Trina almost dropped her act. But if she faltered now, they'd run all over her. Grimly, she pressed her lips together tightly and tried to look fierce. She couldn't believe she was actually pulling this off. But the wide eyes staring at her told her she must sound pretty convincing. "Everyone, outside! We're going to do calisthenics."

Once outside, some of the girls seemed to have recovered from their initial shock at the new Trina. "We want to play," one of the them said.

"You're doing jumping jacks," Trina barked. "Let's go! One, two, one, two . . ."

She put them through the same series of exercises Miss Crawford had directed. At first, they did what they were told. They're actually listening to me, Trina thought with relief. And she tried to ignore the fact that they all looked miserable.

"Now you're going to do push-ups," she ordered.

One girl looked horrified. "On the ground? We'll get our shirts dirty!"

Trina hadn't considered that. For a moment, she hesitated. But the small grin that was forming on Courtney's face recharged her determination.

"Then you'll have to change your clothes. Now get down on the ground and do push-ups."

Slowly, they got into the position. Trina walked among them, examining their efforts. Lisa was barely getting herself an inch off the ground. "You call that a push-up?" Trina asked. "That's pathetic!"

"I can't do push-ups," Lisa whimpered.

"Of course you can! You're just being lazy!"

And then, to her horror, Lisa lowered herself flat on the ground and burst into tears. All around her, the girls were rising, and staring at Trina.

Trina swallowed nervously. "Okay, do sit-ups then."

Courtney stepped forward. "This is free period. We're supposed to be having fun!"

"Too bad," Trina retorted. "I'm in charge and this is what I want you to do."

And then another girl stepped forward. "But this isn't what we want to do."

"Too bad," Trina said again, but she could hear her voice getting weaker. She didn't know how long she could keep up this act.

"And you made Lisa cry," Courtney said. "That wasn't nice of you."

"You—you have to do what I say," Trina said faintly.

Courtney folded her arms. "No."

Trina looked around. They all had their arms folded, and they were all looking at her with the same expression. Trina recognized it. It was the way cabin six had looked at Miss Crawford. The anger and dismay in their expressions said more than words ever could. And that wasn't the way she wanted them to feel about her.

But she had no idea what to do now. With a combination of relief and alarm, she saw their counselor, Karen, coming up the road toward them.

"How's everything going?" Karen asked.

"Fine," Trina managed, and glanced at the girls in trepidation. None of them contradicted her, and she knew why. It was an unwritten law at Sunnyside that campers never went crying to higher authorities. You worked problems out among yourselves. Even nine year olds knew this.

But Karen seemed to sense something was wrong. "You guys look pretty grungy," she said in a cheerful voice. "Why don't you all go in and wash up before dinner?"

Enviously, Trina watched them all respond without argument. Alone with Karen, Trina attempted a smile. "They're—they're nice kids."

"But not always easy to handle," Karen remarked. "Are you having any problems with them?"

79

Trina felt an urge to break down and beg for help. But there was that unwritten law. . . . "No, not really."

Karen eyed her keenly. "Just don't give up. That's what being a CIT is all about—learning. Trial and error. You know what I mean?"

Trina nodded. But how many errors was she going to have to make before she figured out what worked?

As she walked back to her own cabin, she hoped her cabin mates weren't back from their free period yet. She needed some time alone to think.

To her surprise, they were all in the cabin. And they weren't even playing a game. Each girl was lying silently on her own bed.

"What's going on?" Trina asked.

Megan raised her head and put a finger to her lips. "Shh."

From her top bunk, Katie glanced furtively at the closed door leading to the counselor's room. Then, very quietly, she climbed down to Trina's bed, and beckoned Trina to join her.

"We've been grounded," she whispered.

"Grounded? What are you talking about?"

"We were five minutes late getting back from the stables. Five minutes! And that witch told us we'd have to spend every free period for the next week lying on our beds!"

Trina's mouth fell open. "That's—that's outrageous!"

"Shh," Katie hissed. "She'll hear you. She's got ears like a hawk!"

Trina lowered her voice. "But that's not right! If Ms. Winkle knew what she was doing—"

"We can't go tell her, you know that. We have to handle this ourselves." She looked at Trina with troubled eyes. "But how?"

The memory of cabin three's reaction was still fresh in Trina's mind. "I think I know." She turned to the others in the cabin and waved them over. They all looked at the counselor's door nervously. Then, in total silence, they crept off their beds and gathered on Trina's. Whispering, Trina told them her idea.

Katie's eyes widened. "You think that will work?"

Trina sighed. "It's worked before."

Katie was right about Miss Crawford's ears. The counselor's door flew open. "I said no talking! And what are you doing off your beds? Get back to your own immediately!"

Even though the plan was Trina's idea, all eyes flew to Katie. She was the recognized leader of the cabin. And Trina didn't mind letting Katie take the lead one bit.

Katie didn't fail them. Her face may have been

a bit paler than usual, but she rose and spoke clearly. "No."

Miss Crawford stared at her in disbelief. "What did you say?"

"I said, no," Katie repeated. Trina gazed at her in admiration. There wasn't the slightest bit of a tremble in her voice.

The expression on Miss Crawford's face made Trina's stomach churn. "You refuse to obey me?"

"Yes," Katie said. Her courage was contagious. Sarah spoke up. "It's not fair to ground us just because we were late getting back."

"And we don't want to do calisthenics every morning," Megan added.

"Or march everywhere," Erin said. "This is a camp, not an army!"

Trina felt like she had to say something. "Miss Crawford, this isn't how we do things here at Sunnyside. Maybe we can discuss it and—"

"There's nothing to discuss," Miss Crawford barked. "Either you follow my orders or you don't. Which is it to be?"

The girls looked at each other. Then, in unison, they shook their heads.

"This is insubordination! And I will not tolerate it." With that, Miss Crawford went into her room and shut the door.

Megan gazed after her in bewilderment. "What does insubordination mean?"

"I'm not sure," Trina replied. "But whatever it is, she doesn't like it."

Sarah shivered. "What do you think she's going to do to us?"

It didn't take long for them to find out. The door reopened, and Miss Crawford emerged. This time she was carrying a suitcase. She paused only to give the girls one long, scathing look. And then she was gone.

Erin fell back on the bed. "Thank goodness!"

"Wow," Megan breathed. "She gives up easy!"

Katie grinned. "Lucky for us!"

"Trina, what's the matter?" Sarah asked. "Aren't you glad she's gone?"

"Of course I am," Trina said. But at the same time, she couldn't help thinking that the cabin three girls would be just as pleased if she did the same thing.

Chapter 6

The next day, Trina kicked a rock along the path as she walked from cabin three back to her own cabin. Suddenly, she kicked with unusual force, and sent the rock flying into the bushes on the side.

Her head was filled with a jumble of feelings, none of them good. She was mad—at the girls in cabin three, who wouldn't pay any attention to her, and at herself, for not being able to make them listen. She was hurt by the fact that they didn't seem to like her. And she was disappointed in the whole CIT experience. It wasn't what she'd expected at all.

What was she doing wrong? she wondered. Today, she'd tried to coax them into a game. In her mind, she replayed the hour. "Let's go outside and play Simon Says," she'd said to them. They'd all groaned.

"That's a baby game," Marsha complained. And no one made a move toward the door.

"I'll read you a story," Trina offered. Again, there was no response. Trina went over to their little bookcase and selected *The Wind in the Willows*. That had been one of her favorite books when she was nine years old.

She opened it and began to read. It didn't take long for her to realize no one was listening. Two of the girls pulled out a board game and started playing it. The others were talking. One of them took another book and curled up with it.

They acted like she wasn't even there. Trina didn't know what to to do. So she just kept on reading out loud, to nobody. And she was still reading when Karen returned.

You can always quit, she told herself as she walked. But quitting didn't appeal to her. Quitting meant admitting defeat. And she wasn't ready to do that. Not yet. But the thought of day after day with cabin three was making her feel very depressed.

"Hey, Trina!"

She looked over her shoulder. Brandy was running toward her. "Hi," she said breathlessly. "I just left cabin two. And I'm exhausted!"

Trina hadn't had a chance to talk with her since

they both began their CIT jobs. "How's it going in your cabin?"

"Great! They're so cute. I wish I was their real counselor. I could spend all day with those kids. How's it going for you?"

"Terrific," Trina lied. "We're having a super time." She was dying to ask Brandy exactly what she was doing with her campers during the free period. But then Brandy would want to know what *her* group had been doing. And Trina was never very good at keeping up a lie for long.

"You know what they said to me today?" Brandy continued. "They told me they wished I could be their counselor all the time!"

"That's nice," Trina said. "I have to get back to my cabin. See you later." She hurried off with a determined step.

As she approached cabin six, she could see her cabin mates coming from the opposite direction. She ran over to join them. "What have you guys been up to?"

"We had a volleyball game outside with cabin five," Katie reported. "And we won."

Trina could tell they must have put a lot of effort into it. They all looked pretty sweaty. "Megan, what's that all over your shirt?"

"Dirt," Megan replied, and grinned. "I took a couple of falls."

"But you haven't heard the news," Sarah said. "We just saw Donna. She says our new counselor's here." She made a face. "I can't wait to see what this one's like."

Trina tried to sound optimistic. "She can't be any worse than the first two."

"And if she is, we'll just get rid of her," Katie replied. "We're getting to be pretty good at that."

"Well, let's check her out," Erin said in a glum voice. Together, they all went inside the cabin.

The door to the counselor's room was closed. But they could hear music coming from inside the room. Erin's face perked up. "Hey, she must have brought a radio or a cassette player."

They waited for the door to open. "I wonder if she heard us come in," Megan whispered.

Katie pressed her ear against the door. "Maybe not. The music's pretty loud."

"I guess we should knock and tell her we're here," Trina said.

Katie rapped lightly on the door. There was no response. She knocked harder. A voice from inside said, "Yeah?"

"I guess she means for us to come in," Erin said. Katie turned the knob and opened the door.

The girl sitting on the bed had long, brown, fashionably frizzy hair. She wore denim cutoffs and a halter top. She didn't even look up at the

girls. Her attention was focused on her fingernails, which she was carefully polishing bright
red. Her bare feet revealed toenails of the same
color, and they still looked wet.

Katie coughed loudly, and the girl glanced up.
"Hi."

"Hi," Katie replied. "Are you the new substitute counselor?"

"Yeah."

"What's your name?" Megan asked.

"Sandy."

The girls waited for her to ask them their
names. When she didn't, Katie took charge and
volunteered them. "I'm Katie, this is Trina, Megan, Sarah, and Erin."

The counselor wasn't even looking as Katie
made the introductions. How was she going to
know who was who? Trina wondered. She certainly didn't seem very anxious to find out.

"Nice to meet you," she murmured, still concen-
trating on her fingernails. "Could you hand me
that box of tissues on the dresser?"

Erin obliged. "Thanks."

"Have you ever been a camp counselor before?"
Katie asked.

"No."

Trina eyed her curiously. "How come you decided to be one now?"

Sandy shrugged. "This friend of mine is a counselor here, in cabin nine. She told me the director, Miss what's-her-name, needed a substitute for a week. And I needed a few bucks."

"What do you usually do?" Sarah asked.

Sandy actually looked up. "Hey, what is this, an interview or something?"

"We're just curious," Megan protested.

"Well, if you have to know, I'm a student at the university. I've been working as a waitress all summer. But I figured this would be easier. I mean, you guys are old enough to take of yourselves, right?"

"Absolutely," Erin assured her.

Sandy replaced the top on the polish bottle, and waved her hands in the air to dry. "Aren't you kids supposed to be somewhere now?"

"It's just about time for dinner," Sarah reported.

"Okay. See you later."

"Aren't you coming to dinner?" Katie asked.

"My nails aren't dry. I'll be along later."

"I guess I should change my shirt," Megan murmured.

Sandy shrugged. "If you want to." Carefully, so she wouldn't smudge her nails, she picked up a magazine and began flipping through it.

The girls backed out of the room. "Close the door," Sandy called out, and they did.

"Boy, Carolyn would never let me go to dinner looking like this," Megan said.

Sarah had a distinct look of disapproval on her face. "She doesn't act like a counselor."

Erin agreed, but her reaction to this was obviously different. "No kidding! Hey, guys, I think we lucked out this time!"

Over dinner, they discussed the new counselor. "I don't think she's going to give us any trouble," Katie said. "Which is a relief. I'm running out of ideas on how to get rid of counselors."

"Well, she's definitely not the type to make us march and do calisthenics," Sarah said.

"There she goes now," Megan said. They all looked at their new counselor, who walked past their table without even a smile or a wave and joined a couple of other counselors sitting alone at a table.

"She won't care what we do," Erin said. "I have a feeling we can get away with anything now."

"But what exactly do you want to get away with?" Trina asked.

"All those things Carolyn never lets us do," Erin said. "We can get out of doing all those things we never want to do. Like archery. And I'll bet she lets us stay up as late as we want."

"I wouldn't count on that," Trina said. "I mean, she *is* a counselor. I'm sure she's going to follow the usual rules."

All eyes turned to Sandy. Katie studied her thoughtfully. "I'm not so sure about that."

Katie was right. After dinner, they joined the rest of the campers for a movie on the lakefront. When they got back to their cabin, Sandy wasn't even there.

"Let's play Monopoly," Megan suggested.

"It's kind of late to be starting Monopoly," Trina objected. "We'll never finish."

But the others were up for it. They set out the board, dealt the money, and began playing. They got so involved in the game, no one even noticed the time.

When Sandy walked in, Trina looked at her watch and gasped. It was almost eleven! She waited for Sandy to order them into bed.

But she didn't. "I'm going to bed," she announced, and went in her room.

As soon as the door closed, Erin turned to the others with a triumphant grin. "See? I told you she wouldn't care when we go to bed."

"This is unbelievable," Megan said in awe. "I've never heard of a counselor who didn't order lights out."

Trina's forehead puckered. "She doesn't seem to care if we get enough sleep or not."

"So what?" Katie asked. "Look, we have to take advantage of this. When Carolyn comes back, we'll catch up on sleep."

Sarah nodded. "No kidding. Carolyn would never let us stay up this late."

"I *like* this counselor," Erin announced. "Hey, maybe Carolyn won't come back and we'll have her the rest of the summer."

Trina was shocked. "Erin! How can you say that? If Carolyn doesn't come back, it will only be because her mother's not doing well."

"Okay, okay," Erin said. "But think of all the freedom we're going to have now. Like Katie said, we'd better make the best of it, 'cause we won't have it forever."

"I wonder if she likes us," Sarah murmured.

Katie brushed that aside. "Who cares, as long as she leaves us alone?"

Megan turned to Sarah. "I'll bet she won't care if you skip everything and stay in the cabin all day to read."

Sarah brightened at that idea. Everyone knew Sarah would rather read than participate in any camp activities. Carolyn was the one who made her go out and do things.

A yawn escaped Trina's lips. "Sorry."

Katie eyed her sternly. "Don't you go falling asleep on us. It's your turn."

Trina threw the dice, and landed on Chance. She drew a card. " 'Go to jail. Go directly to jail. Do not pass Go. Do not collect two hundred dollars.' " She moved her little thimble into the jail square.

"You can pay and get out right away," Megan reminded her.

"I think I'll just stay there a while and wait till I throw doubles." She'd just as soon be out of the game for a while. It would give her a chance to ponder this new situation they were in.

She'd just seen another completely different type of counselor. And everyone seemed to be happy with her. It was something to think about. . . .

The next morning, Trina had a hard time opening her eyes. Sun streamed into the cabin, but her body felt like it was still the middle of the night. What time had they gone to bed anyway? she wondered. Two?

She rolled over toward the bedpost, where she'd hung her watch. It took her a moment to focus her sleepy eyes on the dial. Then she squinted and stared at it. That couldn't be right.

As the numbers on the dial penetrated her head, she sat up. "Oh my gosh!"

Above her, Katie stirred. "What's the matter?" she asked in a drowsy voice.

"The time!"

Across the room, Megan sat up. Rubbing her eyes, she asked, "What time is it?"

"Nine thirty!"

Erin hoisted herself up on an elbow. "Nine thirty? That's not possible. We're always up by eight."

"That's because we're usually in bed by ten," Trina replied. "We've missed breakfast!"

The word "breakfast" brought Sarah's head up fast. "What did you say?"

"We overslept!" Trina couldn't remember this ever happening in cabin six before. Usually, they all woke up automatically. And if they didn't, there was always Carolyn to make sure they were out of bed and ready for breakfast on time.

Trina got out of bed. She went to the counselor's door and knocked. There was no response.

"She must be sleeping too," Katie said.

Trina knocked again, harder. When there was still no response, she turned the knob, opened the door slightly, and peered inside. "She's not here."

Katie stared at her in disbelief. "She just left while we were sleeping?"

"I guess so." The idea that a counselor could just walk past five sleeping campers and go to breakfast without them made her feel sort of sad. It was as if Sandy didn't care whether they got up or not.

But no one else seemed particularly upset. "I can do without breakfast," Erin said, stretching her arms out. "I feel like I've been gaining weight anyway."

"Yeah, me too," Sarah said. "I just hope they didn't have blueberry pancakes."

Trina just stood there, uncertainly. "Well, I guess we better get ready for swimming. And we need to straighten up for inspection."

"I'm going to wear my bikini," Erin announced. "If Sandy doesn't care about us getting up on time, she won't care about regulation bathing suits either."

They had just finished putting on their suits when Sandy walked in. "We overslept," Megan informed her.

"Oh yeah?" She acted like it was no big deal.

"We missed breakfast," Trina added.

Again, Sandy just shrugged. "I'm going to wash my hair." She started toward the bathroom.

"Uh, what about inspection?" Trina asked.

Sandy looked at her blankly. "Inspection?"

"Never mind," Katie said quickly. "C'mon, you guys, let's go to the pool."

"We won't even have to make our beds!" Erin

exclaimed gleefully as they walked to the pool. "And she didn't say a word about my suit. How does it look?"

She posed in front of them. Trina had to admit that the high-cut bottom and strapless top made Erin look very sophisticated. "Do you think you'll be able to swim in it?" she asked doubtfully.

Erin laughed. "Probably not. I'd be afraid to do any big strokes. I could pop out of this!"

Katie frowned. "But we're doing butterfly strokes today. How are you going to manage?"

"I just won't work very hard at it," Erin replied.

Unfortunately, Darrell had other plans. It was a rigorous lesson that day. And Trina actually felt sorry for Erin, struggling to keep her bathing suit top up while practicing strokes. She looked pretty ridiculous, clutching her top with one hand while flapping the other in the water. Everyone noticed, and kids were laughing at her.

"I guess there's a good reason for having regulation tank suits," Trina remarked to her when the lesson was over.

"Yeah," Erin agreed glumly. "Next time, I'll save this suit for free swim days."

They went back to the cabin to change. "I wonder where Sandy is," Megan said.

"Don't trouble trouble till trouble troubles you," Katie sang out. "Hey, we can skip archery today!"

97

"What do you want to do instead?" Trina asked.

"I'm kind of hungry," Sarah murmured.

"We could go get ice cream," Katie suggested.

The thought of ice cream on an empty stomach wasn't exactly appealing to Trina. But she went with the others to the ice cream stand anyway. "This is great," Megan said. "We can do anything we want to do."

"Let's see if we can take canoes out," Katie suggested.

Trina thought about all the energy it took to row the canoes. "I'm not really up for that."

"Me either," Sarah said.

"What do you want to do then?" Katie asked.

Erin yawned. "Personally, the only thing I'm up for is a nap."

"Yeah, that sounds good to me," Megan said.

Katie looked at them in dismay. "You want to waste our first day of freedom sleeping?" And then she yawned. "Well, maybe that's not such a bad idea after all."

Trina was still feeling a little groggy when she entered cabin three that afternoon. But that didn't matter, since what she planned to do with them didn't require much energy.

The nine year olds were just getting up from

their rest period. "Are we going outside today?" one of them asked her.

Trina did her best imitation of a Sandy-style I-don't-care shrug. "You can do whatever you want." She sat down on a chair in the corner of the cabin and opened the magazine she'd brought with her.

The girls looked at each other, and then turned their eyes to Trina. "Like what?" Courtney asked.

Trina shrugged again. "I don't know. You decide. It doesn't matter to me."

"We could play Red Rover," Courtney suggested.

Lisa looked at Trina. "Can we?"

"I don't care," Trina replied. She pretended to be totally engrossed in her magazine.

The girls headed outside. Trina figured that Sandy would probably just stay here and look at her magazine. But she couldn't go that far. After all, these kids were younger, and they *were* her responsibility.

She went outside, settled herself under a tree, and opened the magazine. But she peered over the pages and watched the girls.

"I'll be captain of one side," Courtney announced. "Casey will be captain of the other side."

"That's not fair," Amber complained. "You two are always captains."

"Yeah," Lisa said, "how come the rest of us never get a chance?"

Trina almost smiled at the sounds of the argument. Courtney reminded her a little of Katie, always wanting to be boss. She didn't always get away with it, though. Carolyn kept her in line.

But Trina refused to get involved. They'd only hate her more for it anyway. When Courtney said she wouldn't play if she and Casey couldn't be captains, the others caved in.

"I'll go first," Courtney said.

"How come you get to go first?" Casey demanded.

"Because."

Trina almost jumped up to suggest they toss a coin or something. But she held back, and once again, Courtney got her way.

Courtney picked Amber for her team, then Casey picked Amy.

"I'll take Lisa," Courtney then announced.

"But that means I have to take Marsha," Casey protested. "I had her last time."

Trina could see why Casey was reluctant to take Marsha. She was the smallest of the girls, and probably not very good at the game.

"Too bad," Courtney said.

"Everyone can break through Marsha," Amy whined. "I don't want her on the team."

Trina could see Marsha's lip trembling, as if she was going to burst into tears. She couldn't blame her. It must feel awful to be unwanted by your own cabin mates.

"I'm not taking Marsha!" Casey shouted.

"Then we can't play!" Courtney yelled back.

Marsha ran back to the cabin. As she passed Trina, the tears were streaming down her face. Trina felt an enormous urge to run into the cabin and comfort her or yell at the others for being so thoughtless. But she didn't do either. She just sat there, staring at the magazine and feeling wretched.

Chapter 7

The volleyball game between cabin six and cabin seven wasn't going very well—at least, not for cabin six. Trina wasn't surprised by her cabin's dismal efforts. After three nights of staying up really late, missing breakfast, skipping activities, and just hanging around the cabin, none of her cabin mates had any energy.

The ball came toward her. Normally, Trina would have run forward to meet it, but she was too tired to move very fast. As the ball flew over her head, she made a feeble effort to reach it, but her jump wasn't as high as it usually was. Behind her, Megan was totally spaced out. At the last minute, she tried to hit the ball, but ended up tripping on her feet and falling for the umpteenth time that day.

The game was over, and their score was so low

it was humiliating. "You guys were really lousy," Katie grumbled as they left the activities hall.

"You weren't so great yourself," Erin retorted. "You missed some really easy shots."

"It's not my fault," Katie muttered. "My timing was off."

"My knee hurts where I fell on it," Megan complained. "I'm going to have a huge bruise."

"You always have bruises," Sarah muttered. "What's one more or less?"

"Let's not fight," Trina suggested in a tired voice, but she knew it was a useless request. It seemed like they were all getting on one another's nerves lately.

The condition of cabin six didn't improve their spirits. "What a mess," Trina murmured. The beds hadn't been made in days. Clothes, games, and a general assortment of stuff lay all over the floor. Nightstands and dressers were coated with a thin layer of dust.

"Has anyone seen the book I was reading?" Sarah asked. "I left it somewhere around here."

"It's probably buried under all your junk," Megan said, eyeing with distaste the pile of damp towels on the floor by their bunk.

"That's your junk too," Sarah retorted.

Even Katie looked a little overwhelmed by the

chaotic state of the room. "Can you imagine what Carolyn would say if she saw this?"

"She'd scream and throw a fit," Erin replied.

"No she wouldn't," Trina said. "She'd just tell us to clean it. And I bet she'd help us too."

There was a moment of silence as the girls contemplated the mess and considered Carolyn's reaction to it. "I wonder how she's doing," Katie said. "I hope her mother's okay."

Erin ran a finger over her nightstand and looked at the resulting smudge in disgust. "I wonder when she's coming back to Sunnyside."

Trina looked at her in surprise. "I thought you were glad she left."

The door to the cabin opened and Sandy sauntered in. "Hi. What's new?"

Trina could tell from her tone that she was just making conversation. She wasn't really interested.

"We lost our volleyball game," Katie reported.

Sandy went over to the mirror and began fiddling with her hair. "Oh yeah?"

"And I hurt my knee," Megan said. "See?" She pointed to the spot where a black and blue mark was forming.

Sandy gave it a fleeting glance. "Uh-huh."

"It hurts," Megan added.

Sandy shrugged. "Go to the infirmary." She examined her hands. "Darn, I chipped my thumbnail." With that, she went into her room and shut the door.

Megan made a face at the closed door. "She doesn't even care."

"It's just a little bruise," Erin pointed out.

"Yeah, but Carolyn would have looked at it. And if I had to go to the infirmary, she would have taken me there."

"Erin, remember when you had that cold last month?" Trina asked. "Carolyn sat by your bed, and read to you, and mixed your aspirin with orange juice so it wouldn't taste so bad."

"You know what I was just thinking about?" Katie plopped down on Trina's bed. "That time we were all fighting about something, I don't remember what. I guess we were all just sort of bored and cranky. And Carolyn took us bird-watching in the forest."

"I remember that," Sarah said. "I thought it sounded like a silly thing to do. But she really got us into it."

Trina wandered over to their little bookcase. She picked up the book Carolyn had used to help them identify birds. Then she spotted another book next to it. The spine read *Wildflowers.* She took it out and leafed through it.

"Carolyn's okay," Erin said. "I know I complained about her a lot but she was really a pretty good counselor."

"I miss her," Megan said.

Carolyn was a good counselor, Trina thought. Firm and even strict when she had to be. But always kind. She cared about them. She wanted them to enjoy themselves, but she made them respect each other too. That was what being a counselor was all about.

She stood very still. A germ of an idea was forming in her mind. And then it began to bloom.

"I have to get over to cabin three," she announced.

"You've still got ten minutes before free period," Katie pointed out.

"Yeah, but I've got something to do first. See you later." And she hurried out of the cabin, clutching the book about wildflowers.

She made a stop at the arts and crafts cabin. After a brief consultation with Donna, she left with six straw baskets hanging over her arms. As she approached cabin three, Karen was coming out. "Hi, Trina," she said. "I've been meaning to ask you, how's it going with my campers? Is it getting better?"

Trina grinned. "Not yet. But it's just about to."

Karen looked at her curiously, but Trina just sailed on past her and went into the cabin. The six girls barely looked up as she entered. But Trina didn't let that bother her. "How would you girls like to go on a treasure hunt?"

She thought she detected a slight sign of interest in at least two faces. She pushed on before she could lose them. Holding up the book she'd brought, she said, "This a guide to wildflowers. A lot of these flowers can be found in the field near the forest. Today, we're going out to that field and see how many of these flowers we can find."

"Sounds boring to me," Courtney stated.

"Oh, I don't think it will be boring at all," Trina went on smoothly. "You see, you'll have to identify each flower by the picture in this book. And it's going to be a competition." She held up her arms with the baskets dangling from them. "Each of you will get a basket. When you locate a flower, we'll look at the book and see what it is. And the person who finds the most flowers wins."

She could have sworn she saw a flicker of interest in Courtney's eyes. "What do we win?"

Bribery was not part of Trina's plan. "Nothing," she said, "except for the glory of knowing you did the best job." Ignoring the fact that no one was exactly leaping off their beds to join her, she went around the cabin and distributed the baskets. "Okay, let's go."

108

One by one, the girls slowly got off their beds, and Trina led them outside.

"Anyone know a good song we could sing as we walk?" she asked. When no one responded, she said, "How about 'I've been working on the railroad'?" And before anyone could protest, or call it a baby song, she threw back her head and started singing, "I've been working on the railroad, all the live-long day!"

Normally, Trina would never walk through the Sunnyside grounds singing at the top of her lungs. But this was no time to be her usual shy self. And she didn't have to sing alone for long. By the time she reached, "Can't you hear the whistle blowing," everyone had joined in.

When they reached the field, she lay the book on the ground and opened to the page with pictures of the flowers. "Okay, everyone take a good look. And start hunting!"

The girls crowded around the book and examined the page. Then they took off with their baskets. Casey spotted a huge clump of daisies right away, and they each grabbed one.

"Very good," Trina said. "But some of these aren't going to be so easy to find, and there won't be so many of them." They ran off in different directions this time. Lisa returned first to Trina, tri-

109

umphantly waving a flower in the air. "Is this in the book?"

Together they examined the page. "It's Queen Anne's lace," Trina announced. "Excellent work!"

"Where'd you find that?" Courtney demanded.

Lisa grinned. "I'm not going to tell you. You have to find it for yourself!"

Courtney scowled at Lisa. "That's part of the game," Trina reminded her. "It wouldn't be much of a treasure hunt if you knew where everything was."

Courtney had to admit that was true. And she went off in search of some Queen Anne's lace herself. With the book in hand, Trina went out into the field and watched them as they scurried about, poring through bushes and wading through weeds.

"Is this something?" Amber asked, holding out a small flower with purple petals.

Trina checked her book. "It looks like a wild violet to me." Happily, Amber tossed it in her basket, and ran back out in search of more flowers.

Trina watched with pleasure as the girls roamed and searched through the field. Every few minutes, one of them came running to her clutching a flower, and waited anxiously for her approval. It was just like the time she and her cabin mates had gone bird-watching with Carolyn.

She kept a particular eye on little Marsha. By

110

now, she'd figured out that Marsha was the scape-goat of the group, the one the others tended to pick on. At that moment, Marsha was staring up at the top of a mound. "I think I see a tiger lily!" she screeched.

Courtney, who was thin and wiry, immediately scampered up the mound and grabbed the lone orange flower. "I've got it!" she screamed down. "It's mine!"

"That's not fair," Marsha yelled. "I saw it first!"

"But I *picked* it," Courtney shot back. "So I get the credit, right?" She looked at Trina for confirmation.

Trina hesitated. It was obvious that Courtney was the leader of this group. If she was ever going to win their friendship, she had to win Courtney. But on the other hand—"Girls, what do you think? Marsha spotted the flower first, but Courtney picked it."

Casey looked at Courtney nervously. "Marsha was the one who actually *found* it."

"That's right," Trina said. "Courtney, what do you think is the right thing to do?"

Courtney seemed torn. She looked hard at the flower in her hand. Then she sighed. "Okay. Here, Marsha."

Trina went over to Courtney and put an arm around her. "That was a very noble thing to do."

Courtney squirmed a little. But Trina could tell by her expression that she was pleased with the compliment. And Trina couldn't help but be pleased with herself for handling this situation just the way a real counselor would.

Trina skipped all the way back to her cabin. Her heart was light, and she felt absolutely terrific. The cabin three girls had actually been reluctant when she told them they had to go back to their cabin. And she could have sworn they were even sorry to see her leave when their own counselor returned.

She had a lot of work to do now. She wanted to plan a whole variety of events and activities for them. And she couldn't wait to get started.

Back in cabin six, the girls were all sitting around, looking bored "What did you guys do for free period?" Trina asked.

"Nothing," Katie said, looking disgruntled. "I wanted us to go canoeing. But we can't take out canoes without a counselor. And Sandy didn't want to go."

Just then, Teddy, the handyman, appeared at the door. "Hi, girls. Is your counselor here? I've got a message from Ms. Winkle for her."

Trina looked at the others. "I don't know. Is Sandy here?"

"She hasn't been out of her room since you left," Erin said. Trina went to her door and knocked.

"Yeah?"

Trina pushed the door open. Sandy was lying on the bed, reading a magazine. "What do you want?" she asked Trina.

"There's a message from Ms. Winkle for you," Trina said. Sandy dragged herself off the bed and padded out into the cabin. She opened the door and joined Teddy on the steps for a minute. Then she came back inside and went into her room.

"What was that all about?" Katie asked.

They didn't have to wait long to find out. A moment later, Sandy reappeared with her suitcase.

"Where are you going?" Megan asked.

"Your counselor's back, so I'm leaving. See ya." And Sandy walked out.

The girls looked at each other in astonishment. "But it hasn't been two weeks!" Sarah exclaimed. "What's going on?"

They leaped off their beds and ran outside. "There she is!" Megan squealed. Over the ridge, they could see Carolyn coming toward them.

The girls raced across the yard to meet her. Carolyn dropped her suitcase on the ground and opened her arms. "Wow! I didn't expect a reception like this!" she cried out as the group practically leaped on her.

"We're just so happy to see you!" Sarah exclaimed.

"How come you're back so early?" Erin asked. "I thought you were going to be away for two weeks."

"My mother's operation was a success," Carolyn told them. "And she's feeling fine." Surrounded by the girls, she walked to the cabin. "Besides, believe it or not, I missed you guys!"

"We missed you too," Megan assured her.

"I hope you guys didn't give your substitute counselor a hard time," Carolyn said.

The girls exchanged looks. Then they all burst out laughing.

"What's so funny?" Carolyn asked.

"It's a long story," Trina said. She opened the cabin door for them. Carolyn walked in with a big smile on her face, but it didn't stay there long.

"Good grief!" She dropped her suitcase with a thud. "What in the world has been going on here? This place looks like a tornado's been through it!"

The girls stood there awkwardly. And they all looked embarrassed. "It is kind of a mess, isn't it," Katie murmured.

"That's putting it mildly!" Carolyn shook her head ruefully. "You guys really did miss me, didn't you? Okay, everyone, let's get to work."

No one objected or complained. Everyone started

picking stuff off the floor and putting it away. Megan got out a rag and started dusting. When the floor became visible, Sarah grabbed a broom and began sweeping. Carolyn moved through the room, helping to make beds and generally clean up.

"I can't believe this," she said. "What's been going on here?"

"It's been kind of . . . *different,* since you left," Trina said.

"I can see that! How did you get along with your substitute counselor?"

"Which one?" Katie asked, her eyes sparkling mischievously.

Carolyn's mouth dropped open. "What do you mean?"

"We've had three," Megan told her.

Carolyn dropped down on a bed and shook her head. "Three? You went through three counselors in one week?"

"It wasn't all our fault," Erin said hastily. "Well, some of it was."

"See, none of them were like you," Katie told her.

Trina could tell Carolyn was trying to look stern, but the smile that crept up on her face ruined it. "I wonder if you guys deserve the cake I brought back for you."

"A cake?" Sarah's eyes lit up. "What kind? Chocolate?"

"What else? Now, tell me what's been going on."

Katie took over. She reported honestly about the tricks they pulled on the first counselor. "But she was a wimp, Carolyn, honestly. She wouldn't have lasted long anyway."

Carolyn still looked disapproving. "It doesn't sound to me like you helped her very much."

"Wait till you hear about the others." Katie went on to describe their other experiences. As she imitated Miss Crawford, Carolyn started laughing. "Well, maybe you guys will appreciate me a little more now."

"Oh, we will," Erin said fervently. "Honestly, Carolyn, we will!"

The room was in reasonable good shape by then. "Okay, everyone, get ready for dinner," Carolyn said. They all raced to the bathroom to wash up, but Trina lingered behind.

"How has your CIT experience been going?" Carolyn asked her.

"Well, it was rough at first. Being a counselor isn't as easy as I thought it would be."

Carolyn grinned. "That's the truth."

"I made a lot of mistakes," Trina continued. "See, I just wasn't sure how a counselor was sup-

116

posed to act. I tried a lot of different ways. But none of them worked. And then, I finally figured out what a counselor should be."

"And what's that?" Carolyn asked.

Trina had a hard time looking her right in the face. "Just like you."

Carolyn didn't say anything. And when Trina raised her eyes, she could have sworn Carolyn looked like she was about to cry. But her voice was steady and calm as she said, "Thanks, Trina. That's the nicest thing you could say to me. Now go wash up for dinner."

Trina joined the others in the bathroom. Everyone still looked a little tired, but no one was arguing, and everyone looked happy. It was easy to figure out why.

Carolyn was back in cabin six. And Trina felt sure no one would be complaining about her again.

At least, not any time soon.

MEET THE GIRLS FROM CABIN SIX IN

CAMP SUNNYSIDE #8
TOO MANY COUNSELORS
75913-6 ($2.95 US/$3.50 Can)

In only a week, the Cabin Six girls go through three counselors and turn their cabin into a disaster zone. Somehow camp without their regular counselor, Carolyn, isn't as much fun as they thought it would be.

Don't Miss These Other
Camp Sunnyside Adventures:

(#7) A WITCH IN CABIN SIX   75912-8 ($2.95 US/$3.50 Can)

(#6) KATIE STEALS THE SHOW   75910-1 ($2.95 US/$3.50 Can)

(#5) LOOKING FOR TROUBLE   75909-8 ($2.50 US/$2.95 Can)

(#4) NEW GIRL IN CABIN SIX   75703-6 ($2.50 US/$2.95 Can)

(#3) COLOR WAR!   75702-8 ($2.50 US/$2.95 Can)

(#2) CABIN SIX PLAYS CUPID   75701-X ($2.50 US/$2.95 Can)

(#1) NO BOYS ALLOWED!   75700-1 ($2.50 US/$2.95 Can)

MY CAMP MEMORY BOOK   76081-9 ($5.95 US/$7.95 Can)